TO TOUCH
THE DEER

TO TOUCH
THE DEER

BY

GUS CAZZOLA

THE WESTMINSTER PRESS

PHILADELPHIA

COPYRIGHT © 1981 GUS CAZZOLA

BOOK DESIGN BY DOROTHY ALDEN SMITH

First edition

PUBLISHED BY THE WESTMINSTER PRESS®
PHILADELPHIA, PENNSYLVANIA

PRINTED IN THE UNITED STATES OF AMERICA
9 8 7 6 5 4 3 2 1

Library of Congress Cataloging in Publication Data

Cazzola, Gus, 1934–
   To touch the deer.

   SUMMARY: Convinced that his mother is dead after a car accident and unable to face life with his new stepfather, Robert runs off into the Pine Barrens and learns the basic principles of survival in the wilderness.
   [1. Survival—Fiction. 2. Pine Barrens (N.J.)—Fiction. 3. Stepfathers—Fiction] I. Title.
PZ7.C299To   [Fic]   81-10452
ISBN 0-664-32684-6   AACR2

To Angela

1

THEY came in the night. Creeping, crawling, sliding through the tall marsh grass hardly stirring the stalks. Silently! The moonless night froze in a tomblike stillness deepened by the far-off shrill of a quail disturbed in its sleep by a night stalker.

Then the lights flashed on. Two at a time in the distance. One pair flashed from beneath a bush, one from high in a pine tree, one from ground level only spitting distance away. They blinked on, slowly at first, like city lights waking up on the far side of a black river. In minutes the outside of Robert's circle glowed with flashing eyes. Large ones and small ones. They knew he was there . . . hiding. Robert pressed his face into the dusty sand beneath the sweet pepper bush. He closed his eyes to make the lights go away. But they did not. They edged closer.

The musky odor of wet fur drenched the area. Robert sniffed once, twice, then gritted his teeth. The smell became overpowering. A smell of decay and hunger.

7

Robert ran his fingers over the ground until they gripped a rock. Leaping up, he hurled the rock into the largest mass of eyes. The yelp shattered the still night air. All the lights went out at once. Robert ran deeper into the Pine Barrens. A half hour later, the dust still clung to his nostrils. His legs weighed one hundred pounds. He could not drag them any farther. He fell in a heap. He did not see the eyes anymore.

The sharp morning sun burned away the eyes and odor. Its warm rays shot through the spidery limbs of dwarf pines, over the thornbushes, and cradled a litter of five baby rabbits in their nest. Their mother, her nose twitching out of control, sat nearby. Normally she would have gathered their morning meal by now. But not this morning. Not with this strange creature so close. She had heard him come in the night. Not silently on soft paws like the fox. Or suddenly in one swoop like the screaming hawk. Just plodding through the underbrush, then CRASH! After a bit, when she sensed no movement, she passed it off and fell asleep. But the strange creature was still there in the morning.

Robert awoke slowly—one eye at a time. The crisp air in the pines tingled his lungs like jabbing pine needles. He sat up with a start. "NO!" he screamed. Remembering his nightmare, he screamed again, "NO!" He had tried so hard to forget the car trip . . . to put it out of his mind completely. The mad run into the woods. The eyes. The night. But nothing blotted it away. The tragic thoughts kept coming back, refusing to stay buried. "NO!"

In a wild frenzy, he grabbed a chunk of wood and tossed it at a sniffing rabbit in the bush. It struck the rabbit on

8

the head. The rabbit shivered once, then lay still. Robert struggled to breathe. Everything was closing in on him. It was his first asthma attack since it had happened. Robert stood over the fallen rabbit, wheezing through his mouth. Stay calm, the doctor had said. He went to kick the animal under the bushes, but something held back his foot.

"Everything has to die!" he yelled to the overhead pines. "Why not you too!" Spinning on his heel, he ran deeper into the woods.

"Mom!" he moaned beneath his breath. But he knew she would not hear him. The pines muffled his cries.

Robert pushed his legs onward. His feet struck the ground like a slow beat of the drums. *Boom! Boom!* One foot after the other. Up and down. He had long since lost all feeling in both legs. His breathing came easier now. One foot followed the other in the same steady beat. His mind spun in a whirlpool. He remembered when his mother and he first came to the Pine Barrens from the city five years ago. He was only a small boy then. It was a nice day, as he recalled. The spiffy salesman did not pause in his sales pitch. He acted like a circus barker.

"Step right up! You'll love the Pine Barrens. One third—I said, one third of New Jersey, and it's just like it was three hundred years ago." This salesman could sell rust to a wooden Indian, Robert had thought. He did not come up for air. "It's so wild that hikers get lost in these woods every year. The Pines just swallows them up . . . out of sight, good-by, and don't forget to write. I said *gone!*" Robert's eyes popped open. His mother gasped. Nervously she tossed her checkbook on her lap, turning pages . . . jotting down numbers. Trying to add money that was not there. The salesman continued his pitch. Unloading the shack meant a healthy paycheck for him. "Right smack in the middle of civilization. Only two hours from New York, or Philadelphia to the west. But here, it is wilderness. You did want to be alone, didn't you, Mrs. Belson?" She nodded, half listening. Robert smiled.

They had bought the decaying house near Munsey, smack on the edge of the Barrens. Nothing but miles of stunted pine trees, sand, and cedar creeks. A maze of dirt roads crisscrossed each other, leading nowhere. Once wagon trails, the roads continued for miles, only to come to dead ends. Maybe a few bricks or a dying foundation of a house that had long since disappeared. Some Pineys still lived at the end of some of the roads, deep in the underbrush. But it is better to wrestle rattlesnakes than to mess with the Pineys. Or so Robert had read. Some travelers did and were never heard from again. The salesman laid it on thick. These folktales added glamour to the property.

After her husband died, Mrs. Belson needed work, and an inexpensive place to live. The Barrens offered both. "And don't play too deep in the woods," she scolded. "You heard what the real estate man said about those missing people."

"Come on, Mom! I could live forever in there," Robert said.

She shook him by the shoulder. "Look, Robert, I've got enough to worry about right now just keeping us together. If you want to help, just promise that you will never—*never*—go to deep into those woods."

Robert bit his lip. Why doesn't she understand? She

10

knows that I took survival training at summer camp for three straight years while Dad was ill. She knows that I know the names of every bush and animal in these woods. He nodded to her. "O.K., Mom . . . I promise."

"I promise!" He caught himself yelling out loud, alone now in the woods. "Gotta stop that!" he moaned. "Don't panic—calm down."

Robert stopped where a thick line of scrub pines bordered an open clearing. A log cabin was in the center of an overgrown field of daisies and clover. A wavy metal roof rusted beneath the sun. A Piney shack! Maybe some old hermit!

Robert crouched by a tree. He heard a muffled rustle of leaves to his right. He froze.

There . . . again. He heard it again. He decided to circle the clearing shack and leave it behind him. He was in no mood for people. He was in no mood for questions. He made a mental note of its location should he ever need it. Some tall pines, a sycamore tree not native to the area. Good enough, he thought. Not that he would ever need their help. He did not need anyone's help.

By midday his stomach began to growl. He gobbled some raspberries, the red juices running down the sides of his mouth. He moved to wipe his mouth with the back of his hand, but stopped short. No need to! No need for manners anymore. It is just the wilderness and me. He laughed. The land did not change. The pines and sand rolled on for miles like the empty sea. Occasionally a cedar creek crossed his path. The water felt refreshing and cold. Colder than any tap water, he thought.

11

He climbed the tallest tree he could find. The rough bark felt sharp against his cheek, but scratched his city thighs. They were soft and untested. He still wore his cutoffs and T-shirt, which had the message *I Am The Greatest* blazed across the front. No need to wear more. It was to be just a simple family outing to Pine Lake before it had happened.

"If I'd have known, I would have brought my knapsack . . . even a tent." But he had not known. How could he have known? It had happened so quickly. His chest tightened like a clamp. He struggled to breathe. He tried to think about something else.

Like, Where am I?

Robert locked his arms and legs around the tree trunk, twisting his head in all directions. He saw nothing but a sea of green . . . rising and falling like the Atlantic Ocean off to the east. He made out the Jersey shore. He decided to head west, away from the crowds of people. Away from towns and deeper into the Pine Barrens.

At the base of the tree, he sank his head beneath the rust-colored waters of a small creek. Coming up for air, he hardly recognized the face reflected in the water. His curly hair was clogged with briers and pine needles. Dust coated his eyelids. He blinked his blue eyes in disbelief. He ran his fingers across the corners of his mouth.

"You will make it!" he snapped to the watery image. The image snapped back, "You will make it!"

Robert followed the stream to a depression in the land. It was the closest thing to a valley in the Barrens.

There were no mountains, few hills, and less rolling land. He yanked up a cattail by its root in the ankle-deep marsh and washed off the mud. With his penknife, he peeled the root until it was fleshy white. He chewed on it. Once cleaned and boiled, it looked like a potato. The Lenni-Lenape Indians thrived on it while they waited for their corn to grow. It tasted bitter.

Gri-bit! sounded to his left. Robert froze. Bullfrogs! His mouth watered. He had not realized just how hungry he was. Two days of running does work up an appetite. Quietly, Robert slid toward the sound. *Gri-bit!* He raised his feet just high enough to clear the bottom mud and pushed them forward to the next foothold. He parted the tall cattail shoots. The bullfrog sat on a half-submerged log. Robert crept closer. The frog sensed danger. It stopped croaking; its tongue flicking in and out for information. Robert tossed the chewed root of the cattail behind it.

Splash! As expected, the frog leaped in the opposite direction. Right into Robert's arms. He bundled its wiggling body inside his T-shirt. It tickled. His T-shirt did a disco dance.

His next victim was smaller. With a long stick he whomped that frog across the side of the head. Inside his shirt, that frog did not move. It just lay there. Robert zonked two more before climbing onto dry land. Four frogs in all. "Nice haul for a city kid!"

Robert's stomach growled. His mouth rippled like a wavy line. Jamming his hand into his back pocket, he heaved a sigh of relief. He pulled out a discolored book of matches. He had carried them for the Fourth of July

13

celebration, figuring to pop off a few firecrackers. But he never had.

Carefully he made a small tepee of pine needles and twigs. He gathered thicker pieces of wood and, after snapping them into six-inch lengths, laid them beside his fireplace. With one stick he cleared an area down to the bare ground. He lit one soggy match, and it sputtered out. Another. Then another. The next one held its flame and he thrust it into the tepee. The flames shot upward. He added more wood to the fire. Once satisfied, he cracked some green twigs from a nearby oak tree and peeled off the bark. After sharpening one end, he speared a frog's leg on one stick. He propped the stick at an angle over the fire, burying the other end in the ground. He did this with each leg. Soon eight legs roasted over the fire. As the flesh browned, he turned the legs over like marshmallows. He could not wait. They tasted better than his last ice-cream sundae.

After dinner he cupped a handful of cedar water. It was dark in color, but as clean as a mountain stream. He leaned against a tree with hands behind his head. What a life, he sighed! The crisp smell of burning oak filled the air. Pure clear water filled his throat. Plump, mouth-watering frog's legs filled his gullet.

A rustle in the bushes woke him from his daydream. He decided to push on while he still had some daylight left. The deer runs became less open now in this deep section of woods. Branches slapped at his face. Ruts lined the runs. Deer followed the same paths to and from water. Even after housing developments sprang up overnight across their runs, the deer still followed

14

their ancient paths, like their parents before them. From his window, Robert had watched how confused they became, their large black eyes searching for a path no longer there. They pawed the asphalt, and cringed their noses at the strange aromas of barbecued hamburgers. Some were struck by cars. Others—the lucky ones—found new runs or a different water supply.

The runs were not as noticeable as a sidewalk, but they were there—if you knew what to look for. Trampled leaves, deer droppings. To Robert, the run looked like a major highway. He prided himself on his Indian skills. Best in school, his teachers said. But in the failing light, the run all but disappeared into the underbrush.

In the distance, Robert saw a shadow with straight lines. He stopped. Nature did not grow straight lines. Even tall cedars were slightly twisted. Straight lines usually meant one thing. Man! Flopping on his stomach, he crawled forward through the leaves. There in a small clearing surrounded by a large oak tree stood a house. No, a shack!

His ears froze like the ears of a well-trained hound dog. No smoke rose from the chimney. No dogs howled outside. He saw no burning candles, but he did not want to chance it. People meant questions, and questions meant trouble. He would check it out in the morning.

Robert hoped that the eyes of the night stood clear of shacks. He formed a pillow of oak leaves beneath his head. He was bushed. He covered himself with a few handfuls of leaves to keep away the night chill. His bones ached.

15

As he drifted off to sleep, he saw himself as an Indian brave running along a deer run, his nose following the scent. He wished he had lived in those days before cars. There were no car accidents then. He did not think of his mother as he fell into a restless sleep. But he dreamed of her that night in cold chills and fever.

2

THE tree swallow dove from the branch, leveled off two feet above the ground and snagged the moth on the wing. She returned with her prize to the tree. The moth fluttered in her bill, but she held fast. Her fledglings— three in all—teetered on the branch, hanging on for dear life. The largest one made a grab for the moth. The mother pulled back, as if to say, You're on your own now, kid. She swallowed the moth in one gulp. The fledglings looked downcast. She wanted to help, but they had to learn. They had to survive on their own. With her wing, she knocked the largest chick off the branch.

It fell straight down. The mother yelled instructions. It flopped; it fluttered. Feathers flew in all directions. Harder! Harder! Finally the outstretched wings grabbed air, and the chick swooped over the ground like a Frisbee. Feeling confident, it tried to bank right, but the left wing tip dipped too low. The chick fell straight down . . . down, and landed on the chest of an intruder, who was all but hidden beneath a bed of leaves.

17

Robert's eyes flew open. Seeing the bird, he slammed an open hand against his chest, nearly knocking himself out. But, urged on by the overhead chatter, the chick shot up like a rocket. The fledglings followed their mother away from the danger zone. They quickly learned to fly.

Robert sat up. He dragged the sleepers from his eyes. With an arm he rubbed the cold sweat from his forehead. Another restless sleep! Another terrifying nightmare!

He parted the underbrush to get a better view of the house in the distance. "It has to be a hunter's shack, " he said to himself, "like the one near my home." Robert scratched his head. But so far back in the woods? At one time big-city hunters had formed hunting clubs. They all chipped in cash to build shacks for their yearly deer hunts. Sometimes they left a caretaker. But it makes no sense, Robert puzzled. That was years ago. Now hunters roared through the woods in four-wheel drives and motorcycles. No need for hunting shacks. The hunters drove home before the deer turned cold.

Robert checked the entrance. No tracks. No telltale footprints. Months of rain and wind had erased the last signs of man. The shack had to be deserted. Robert crouched, Indian style, and moved into the opening. His toes felt for branches before touching down. He paused against the corner of the shack, his back pressed tightly against its cedar siding. It had weathered to a light gray. The house sat on four cinder blocks, one at each corner. There were no windows. Only shutters, one of which hung loosely on one hinge like a broken doll. Robert listened to his thumping heart. He heard no other sound.

The door squeaked open just a few inches. A fist of air

blasted his face. A small wet nose shoved its way through the opening near the floor. A dog's nose? Definitely an animal of some kind!

Robert gasped in horror. The body behind the nose was black and white.

"Oh, no!" he yelped. "A skunk!"

The skunk shuffled through the doorway, hardly raising its eyes. It thrust its head over its shoulder toward Robert as if to say, Nice day we're having. Robert dared not move. He gritted his teeth. Keep that tail down! The skunk waddled away from the shack. Robert hissed a long sigh of relief.

Still pressing his back against the shack, he eased open the door with his left hand. The rusty hinges creaked in protest. He waited a moment. Hearing nothing, he stepped inside the doorway.

A large column of musty air slammed into his face. Robert coughed and cleared his eyes. The inside of the cabin was dark. Cobwebs covered the rough-hewn table and chairs. Hornets buzzed in the corner of the ceiling. The cabin was small. It measured four strides deep by three strides across. Robert stood 5 feet 7 inches, and just cleared the ceiling.

A small table, probably made from the stand of young cedars nearby, sat in the center of the room. Two chairs, one with a missing leg, bracketed the table. A makeshift bunk with a mattress woven of thick rope filled the corner. A wooden box sat beneath the bunk. A shelf lined the west wall. On it were rusted coffee cans, moldy cardboard boxes, and a few spent cartridges.

A thick layer of dust coated everything, except for some

paw marks on the floor. No one had lived here for years. Robert rubbed his hands together and yelled, "Home, sweet home!" He opened the shutters to let in some fresh air and sunshine. It was dirtier than he had thought.

He made a broom by tying cedar branches around a long stick. It not only worked well, but it smelled great. He grabbed a metal bucket that was upended in a corner. Filling it with water from a nearby creek, he raced back to the cabin. Half the water leaked out. A Swiss cheese bucket, he laughed. The broom doubled as a mop. He lost all track of time cleaning his new home. He thought of celebrating Christmas in it, and how he might decorate it. A full spruce tree in the corner. He could string dried berries and nuts on it. Maybe some holly branches with red berries on the outside door.

Before long, the cabin sparkled. Robert sat down on the mattress, which quickly snapped in two. The rope was old and moldy. He plopped on the box beneath the bed. His curiosity got the best of him. He pulled the box to the center of the floor. It was locked. He searched around for a tool of some sort to break open the padlock. Junk rusted everywhere outside. Beer cans, spring mattresses. Thinking, I'll clean this mess later, he found a tire jack and brought it inside the cabin. Two shots opened the lock.

He felt like a kid with a new toy. Like that Christmas Eve before Dad died when he had opened his gifts beneath the tree. Green Ghost and Monopoly! He shrugged it off and opened the heavy lid. His mind boggled at its contents.

"Everything I need," he gulped. A rusting Boy Scout

ax, an L. L. Bean hunting knife with a 7-inch blade, some shotgun cartridges, a flint-and-steel kit for making fires, and some needles and thread. Even two worn books: *The Deerslayer*, by James Fenimore Cooper, and *Living off the Land*, by James Lame Bear, a Lenni-Lenape Indian.

Closing his eyes and lifting his head to the ceiling, Robert offered a silent thanks to the Indian spirit who watched over him. Someone had to be watching over him, he reasoned. Such luck did not just happen. He pictured the spirit standing outside like some giant phantom Hiawatha, watching over him and smiling. A rush of cold air swirled through the room. It was gone as quickly as it had come.

"Thanks!" Robert repeated.

A chill iced his spine. Without opening his eyes, he stood up in the center of the shack. He tore off his T-shirt and threw it on the floor. He tore off his cutoffs, kicking them on the pile. He removed his sneakers and socks, and threw his socks on the pile. He tossed his sneakers on the bed for later. He stood naked except for his swim trunks.

A mysterious wind spun around his head, carrying with it bits of crumbled leaves and ancient dust particles. Goose bumps popped over his body. He kept his eyes tightly shut . . . afraid of what he might see. Again the strange wind whistled through the open shutters and up the chimney. His breath caught in his throat. His heart pounded inside his ears. The pounding grew louder, like distant drumbeats. Indian drums stretched with deer hide. Like the beating drums of the Indians three hundred years ago. Tears dribbled from the corners of his eyes. Then the beating stopped.

Robert opened his eyes, feeling somewhat light-head-ed. He cupped the pile of discarded clothes in both arms and threw them in a heap outside. He spread dry twigs and branches over the pile and set fire to it with his last match. The bonfire erupted in one quick burst of energy like a bolt of lightning, its shimmering heat waves reaching for the sky. He wanted to dance. Looking around, he slapped his head, disgusted with himself.

"Why not? I can do what I want now. There's no one around for miles to stop me."

He grunted out the beat of the drums deeply within his throat. BOOM! Boom! LOUD—soft! LOUD—soft! He began slowly, bringing his left toe down softly on the LOUD beat. He brought his left heel down hard on the soft beat. Right foot, left foot. A sacred Indian dance. Or close enough to it, he thought. He circled the fire of burning clothes until all remains of his past life tumbled into gray ashes. He held up his outstretched arms, palms up, to the treetops.

"Whoever you are! Whatever you are . . . I thank you. Robert is no more. I am now . . ." He thought for a moment, then continued. "I am now—Deerslayer! From this day forward, I am Deerslayer who will keep your faith and serve you well. Deerslayer! Deerslayer!" He liked the sound. "I have no mother but *you*. I have no father but *you*. You are my mother and father. I am your son . . . Deerslayer. And Deerslayer *will* survive!" He fell on the ground, exhausted.

A slight breeze from the east woke him. The sun was sinking fast. He rubbed his stomach in hunger. Getting the knife from the cabin, he entered the surrounding underbrush in search of food. Off to his right, five squirrels chattered in some family dispute. He crawled the remaining ten yards to the large oak tree.

The squirrels skittered up and down and around the trunk. One squirrel eyed Deerslayer suspiciously. They were not people shy, this deep in the woods. Deerslayer held the knife ready, and leaped forward. The squirrel easily sidestepped him. Another one was trapped on the ground to Deerslayer's left. He threw his knife at it, but missed by a mile.

It took ten minutes to find the knife in the leaves. He grunted in disgust. Turning, he stopped short at the base of the tree. There lay a squirrel, its throat neatly cut.

Deerslayer gasped in surprise. "I didn't do that. Am I flipping out so soon?" His asthma came back. He doubled over, trying to catch his breath. Slowly, haltingly, his breathing returned to normal. He held the dead squirrel by the tail. Its throat was cut all right. By a knife!

He watched the slow trickle of blood. Blood fascinated him. A fascination with the forbidden and the unknown, like walking into a teachers' room. But it also disgusted him. His stomach knotted, but he fought it off.

Some Deerslayer who can't stand the sight of blood! he thought. He stuck his thumb in the blood and smeared two lines on his face from the corners of his eyes to a point below his mouth. It felt warm. Once alive! He tried to feel its life, its energy. He smeared the rest of the blood on his bare chest. It looked like war paint.

"I am at war," he yelled. "It's kill or be killed here!" He spoke to the treetops, but no one spoke back.

Back at the cabin, he moved with a newfound energy.

He did not question the strange appearance of the squirrel. Instead, he blew a burning ember to life and added more wood. He decided to cook outside. With his ax, he cut three long saplings and tied them together at one end with a strip of bark. He placed the tripod over the growing fire. Filling two coffee cans with water, he hung them on the tripod with two notched sticks. Shaky, but it would do. He held the squirrel on a log between his legs. He closed his eyes as he made the first cut. The rest came easier. He chopped whatever meat he could find into small pieces. He dumped these into the boiling water.

Holding both hands behind his head, he stretched away the cramps. "Seasoning—I need seasoning!" He uprooted some wild onions and diced them into the stew. He dug up the small, scented roots of a sassafras tree, and cleaned them in the creek. He dumped these into the second coffee can for tea. He knew that the Indians used sassafras tea as medicine. He just liked its flavor.

By nightfall, dinner was ready. He ate it slowly this time, enjoying each swallow. The wild onions bit his lip—a sharp taste that took some getting used to. The meat tasted like a meal fit for a king. Or an Indian chief. He ate with his eyes half closed. Never before had a meal tasted so great. The sassafras tea made his stomach gurgle. Even without milk and sugar, it too was out of sight. He sat dreamily after his meal. No need to rush. No need to do anything.

"I'm not going anywhere," he sighed.

As he threw a handful of dirt over the fire, he thought he heard a rustle in the bushes behind him. The blue jays had stopped their constant chattering. Nothing moved.

He strained his eyes into the blackness, but saw nothing.

Then and there he decided to sleep inside that night. Lying on the broken bunk with both hands behind his head, he stared at the blank ceiling. He felt frightened. He shoved the knife under the bed within easy reach. His mind raced. The black ceiling turned red. Red for blood! The squirrel's blood. He shivered, since he knew what was coming next. Red for blood! His mother's blood. He tried to fight it, but the memory returned on its own. The film replayed.

"Pine Lake, again!" Russ Kochak, Robert's new father, snapped to his wife beside him. "We go there every weekend." Robert's mother did not answer.

Robert stood up to him. "What's wrong with Pine Lake? We used to go there all the time."

Russ stared him down. "That was before. Now you go where I want to go. Keep your nose out of this, Robert. You're just a kid." Russ mumbled beneath his breath, then reconsidered. "O.K., we'll go this time. But it's the last time, you understand?"

Robert's mother looked up. Her lips were pale, her face downcast.

The ride to Pine Lake in Russ's '59 Chevy was boring. Robert sat in back with his new sister, Aimee. A little brat. Up front, Russ turned to Robert's mother. "I try to get along with the kid, but he's so . . . thick. You know what I mean?"

Her hand flew to her mouth. "Shhh! He's right behind you. He's very sensitive you know."

"I don't care if he does hear me," Russ yelled to the

roof. "He's got to meet me halfway. It's not easy for me either."

Bearing down like a derailed express train, the Cadillac skidded across the center lane from the opposite direction. It smashed into the left front of the Chevy. The fender crumbled like cardboard. The four occupants of the Chevy lunged forward in their seats, but the safety belts held three of them back. Robert's mother had not fastened her seat belt. Her head smashed into the windshield. The Chevy veered out of control and plowed into a wooden sign off the side of the road. Time froze. Only the dust and the smoke and the steam moved.

After everything settled down, Robert unstrapped himself and tumbled to the ground. Aimee cried in the backseat. Russ cursed up front. But Robert did not hear them. He was staring at his mother. She lay sprawled on the road, half in and half out of the car. Blood poured from her head cuts, forming a pool of red on the asphalt. She did not move.

"Mom!" Robert yelled. "MOM!"

No reply!

Robert screamed. A flock of crows winged into the air from atop a tall pine tree. A few laughing gulls squawked back. Robert ran down the embankment and disappeared into the cedar swamp.

Another rotten rope snapped in his mattress. Deerslayer banged his head against the floor. He could not get the accident out of his mind. It kept repeating over and over like an instant replay.

Deerslayer tried to blink away his mother's bleeding

face, but it only grew larger and larger . . . until it filled the entire cabin with red. He rolled over and shook. He did not want to, but he cried himself to sleep again. Some Deerslayer, he thought. He did not smell the thin wisp of smoke blowing in from the south. It was still five miles away.

3

ONE hundred fathers and one hundred sons encircled the smoking barbecue pit at the Annual Father and Son Big Eat on the back lot of Munsey's Royal Order of the Moose, Lodge 786. They came from miles around.

One hundred fathers! Real fathers, second fathers, Big-Brother fathers, weekend fathers, guilty fathers, make-believe fathers, new fathers, old fathers, and two grandfathers.

One hundred sons! Real sons, second sons, Little-Brother sons, weekend sons, foster sons, unwanted sons, bitter sons, smart sons, and dumb sons.

"How's the chicken?" Russ Kochak, seated on the grass across from Robert, squirmed in his bargain shorts from K-Mart. He smelled of stale tobacco and perspiration. He slapped a centipede that crawled up his hairy leg. The chicken was tasteless.

Robert grunted.

Russ groaned. "Robert," he said slowly, deliberately,

"I asked you if you liked the chicken. You can at least answer me that, can't you?"

Robert tore off a large chunk of meat with his teeth. Can't answer with a mouthful of food. That'll keep him off my back for a few seconds at least, he thought. With head bowed, he stared at the man—no, the stranger—seated across from him. Russ Kochak! What a weird name! Does he think he's a detective or something? Robert laughed inside. The guy looks so funny in that dumb T-shirt and with that potbelly. Forget it! And who wears blue socks and shoes to a barbecue? He threw back a grunt. "It's O.K. . . ."

"Russ! Why don't you call me Russ?"

Robert swallowed hard. Without answering, he jumped to his feet. "Can I have seconds?"

"Sure!" Russ frowned. "But they're having the three-legged race now. We can eat later."

Father and son walked to the starting line, side by side but miles apart. Nervously Russ looked at the other men.

A jolly Moose, red-faced and a little drunk, threw an inner tube at Russ. "You and the kid get into this and line up. Be quick about it."

Russ slipped the inner tube over his right ankle. Robert did not move.

"Come on, Robert. Get into the spirit of the thing. At least try."

Robert frowned. He slipped his left foot inside the tube, next to Russ's foot. He winced when Russ wrapped an arm around his shoulder. He took one look at the hand, then up at Russ. How could Mom allow this to happen?

29

How could she let me go on a dumb picnic with this . . . this . . . weirdo?

"On your mark, get set, GO!" Father and son shot from the starting line. After two hops, their legs entangled; they fell.

"Get up!" Russ yelled, getting into it. Again they tried, but quickly fell behind. Russ went left, Robert went right. Russ went up, Robert went down. Then they both went down . . . this time for good. Russ cursed out loud, then, frowning, said to Robert, "Forget about it. It's O.K. Let's get that chicken."

"I don't feel like any chicken now," Robert sneered. "When are we going home?"

"We just got here. Come on, give it a chance, Robert. It's new for me too, you know. I'm not used to boys. I only had Aimee."

Robert nodded. "Yeah!"

"Let's get some gloves and throw a baseball around. You do like baseball, don't you?"

Robert nodded his head up and down.

Russ crouched about ten paces from Robert. "O.K., hotshot, whiz one in here." He pounded his fist into the open mit. Robert threw a soft lob that plopped into Russ's mit like yesterday's Jello. "Come on, put some pepper behind it," Russ yelled. Robert threw the next one a little faster.

"Faster, boy! Faster!"

You want a fast one? Robert thought. You'll get a fast one, Potbelly. He gave two short pumps, then reared back his leg. Wham! The ball sailed three feet over Russ's outstretched glove and into a boiling pot of beans. The hot sauce splattered three cooks and one hungry dog.

"What kind of pitch is that?" Russ screamed. "Didn't your father ever teach—" He stopped short. Too late! Throwing down his glove, Robert ran.

Russ trailed behind, his mouth wide open, sucking in air. Red-faced, he wheezed to a stop by the weeping willow tree at lakeside. Robert sat beneath the willow, staring at the white swans in the middle of the lake. Getting his breath back, Russ squatted next to Robert. He started to speak three times before the words came out. "Look . . . er-r-r, I'm sorry. I was out of line."

Robert did not respond.

Russ went on. "I got embarrassed back there, that's all. The guys are going to rib me about getting soaked in beans, you know." No reply. Russ begged with open palms. "Look, I don't expect you to love me, or even like me. I know that I can never be like your father."

Robert looked up. "Right!"

"But give me a break! That's all I'm asking. We have to work this out together. You and me." Robert threw a pebble at the swan. The swan flip-flopped to the other side of the lake. Russ sprawled, full length, on the ground beside Robert. "You do love your mother, don't you?"

Robert poked his finger in his ear. He shook his head. "She betrayed me."

"Betrayed you? What do you mean?"

Robert looked right into Russ's eyes, then turned away. "I trusted her, but she let me down."

"I don't understand," Russ said.

"You wouldn't!"

"But you still love her . . . right?"

"I guess," Robert said.

"Well, after your dad died, she needed a friend."

"She had a friend." Robert jabbed his thumb into his chest. "Me!"

Russ shook his head. "No, I mean a friend more her own age. Someone interested in her kind of things."

"She has friends at work. The other waitresses. She has a lot of friends."

"You're making this difficult, Robert. You know what I mean. Do I have to spell it out for you?"

Robert watched an ant run in circles between his feet. He squashed it with his thumb.

Russ broke the silence. "Well, she married me. Doesn't that mean anything?" Robert tightened his lips as Russ nearly shouted. "Give it a try for her sake then."

They sat in silence for a long time. Not looking at each other, just staring across the lake. Robert tossed another pebble at the swan, who by now gave up and flew to another pond. Russ tried a different move. "Do you like animals, Robert?"

Without thinking, Robert answered. "I love animals. Dad and I used to go camping, and—"

Russ leaped to his feet. "Look, you're going to have to stop thinking about the past. I know it's hard, but life does go on."

Robert turned to run. This time Russ grabbed him by the shoulder. "You're not going to run away this time. You just can't just keep running away from this. You're going to listen to me. Your dad is gone, Robert. GONE! He's never coming back. You have to accept that."

"NO!" Robert screamed.

32

Russ looked over his shoulder. "Keep it down, kid. People are looking."

"NO!" Robert screamed again. His breath caught in his throat. Another asthma attack! Russ shook him by the shoulders. "I'm your dad, now!" he yelled. "Whether you like it or not, I'm your dad now."

"Never!" Robert spun from Russ's grip and ran. The smell of barbecued chicken drifted over the lodge grounds. The smell of burning meat knifed through Robert's chest.

The first thing Deerslayer noticed was the smoke. It was thick inside the small shack. Deerslayer fell to his knees and crawled to the door. He coughed. Once outside he looked around. Smoke filled the air. He heard the crackling of burning pine.

Overhead, the crown fire raced through the treetops. Nearby trees burst into flames from the intense heat. The bubbling sap popped like exploding firecrackers. Timber crashed to the ground on all four sides. Deerslayer dove into the creek. Its waters—now warm—had bits of burning twigs floating on the surface. The flames blocked everything from view. He plunged his head underwater.

The thirsty pines became a tinderbox in the summer. The fallen needles, which snapped between the fingers, burned like gasoline. The dry forest just needed one match, one bolt of lightning, one discarded cigarette. Once ignited, twisting flame bulldozed the country-side—out of control.

At Munsey, the volunteer fire fighters worked

feverishly. Backfires did not work. Fire trucks pumped hundreds of gallons of water onto the trees. The fire drank it right up. Helicopters from nearby Lakehurst Naval Air Station spread long streams of chemicals over the burning Barrens. But it was futile.

Deerslayer clung to the bottom mud of the cedar creek. It was only two feet deep at its deepest. The mud let go with a sucking sound. Finally he grabbed a twisted root and held fast. Burning branches and sparks rained down on the water. Then he remembered the box. "I have to get that box," he gurgled—half choking.

Releasing his grip, he popped to the surface. With one forearm across his eyes and the other in front of him, he stumbled to the cabin. Its roof smoldered; its shutters were engulfed in flames. He hotfooted it across the floor. He grabbed the box from beneath the bed, but quickly let go. The metal handle burned his hand. He took a piece of rope from the mattress, and looped it through the handle. He ran outside, dragging the box behind him.

Once clear of the shack, he stumbled, crawled, and tripped to the creek. He pulled the box into the cooling waters. It sizzled. A burning branch, as thick as his upper arm, crashed across his shoulder. He yelped in pain, and fell into the creek. The waters soothed the burning skin, as he felt for the submerged root . . . his anchor against the fire.

The fire growled above him. At its height, it did not crackle or pop. It roared through the trees like a hurricane of flames. Beneath the water on his back, Deerslayer gritted his teeth. He surfaced for air every minute. The hot air burned his throat.

He lay still until the height of the fire passed over. Then, sitting up in the creek, he opened his eyes. Clumps of fire still burned. Smoke rose from the ground. But it curled straight up. He knew that the worst was over, unless the wind shifted.

"Aghhh!" he moaned, grabbing his shoulder. It was swollen and bleeding. The pain was unbearable. The skin had cracked open and already had begun to blister. He smeared the cool bottom mud over the wound. It felt refreshing. After pulling the box from the water, he turned to the shack.

A thin column of smoke rose where once a house had stood. Walls and roof and table and bed were all reduced to ashes.

"First my mom, and now this?" Deerslayer looked into the blue sky and watched a few wisps of cumulus cloud drift by. He remained silent. In the distance to the east, the fire roared toward the shore area. Deerslayer decided to head west. Carrying the precious box, he followed the creek. The burning ground still smoked, too hot to walk on. Splashing through the mud was difficult, but he pushed on.

"That Piney shack!" he thought. "Maybe they'll help me." But deciding otherwise, he narrowed his eyes. "No, I don't need anyone."

Deerslayer gagged at the sight of the burned bodies of helpless birds and animals, trapped in the fire. He stumbled in the water for hours, until green trees slowly replaced black trunks. Until living bushes replaced dead branches. Until insects and birds again filled the air. He left the creek, dragging his box behind him.

The trees still smoked. From a slight rise, Deerslayer looked across a long, low depression filled with spiked grass. His eyes lit up. There, about two hundred yards away, was a hill, not too high, but sparkling like an emerald. He trotted down the rise. A log snagged his foot, and he somersaulted to the bottom. The box banged after him, coming to rest against a laurel bush. His shoulder ached. The mud began to peel away, showing an ugly red gash.

Deerslayer pulled himself and his box to the top of the hill. The summit sparkled with wild flowers of every color. White daisies and golden fluffs of dandelion nodded in the gentle evening breeze. Blooms of red clover highlighted clusters of white blossoms. Delicate angel's breath waved over tiny blue petals and satiny sphagnum moss. Beneath the encircling pines, spicy wintergreen crept upon and beneath the decaying peat. Its white, bell-shaped flowers rang from the tips of fragile branches.

Clusters of inkberry, with dark evergreen leaves, painted the ground. Small pink orchids dotted the lowlands, while blueberry bushes grew along the edges. The sweet perfume of the white pepper bush made his head spin.

To the east, Deerslayer watched the forest fire swallow everything in its path in one shifting line like a black tidal wave. To the west, he blinked his eyes against the setting sun. He marveled at the rolling flatness of green. Here and there large stands of oak and cedar broke the flatness. Squawking crows dotted the orange sky. He sank to his knees, crying out to an unseen spirit. "You are my mother. You are my father. You have led me here. I thank you."

The base of the hill rippled with patches of raspberry vines like curly hair around the ears of a balding man. Small-game animals scurried back and forth, exploring their new home. A rabbit nearly ran into him. The fire had also burned the animals' homes. Deerslayer smiled at their antics. He did not pick up a stick. He did not toss rocks at the squirrels. He felt close to them now. They had survived the ordeal together.

Halfway down the hill, Deerslayer saw a large pine tree, torn up by its roots. Its bushy top on the ground formed a living cave of branches. He looked into the tangled mass.

He stopped short at the sight of the two deer. Lying on their sides, they didn't move. Their chests rose and fell ever so slightly. Their tongues hung down the sides of their mouths, gasping for air. A weird gurgling sound rose from their throats. Both looked nearly dead.

4

BOTH deer glistened with perspiration and looked as frightened as two cats in a roomful of rocking chairs. A lump rammed itself into Deerslayer's throat. He had seen deer before in a zoo behind wire fences. He had seen them in the woods, flashing by a barberry bush, standing concealed in a stand of cedars, or sipping creek water. They always moved with ears tilted upward, alert for danger—like a fox—or with white tails bobbing behind them, once on the run.

But he knew them best by their tracks along the runs. Cloven hooves dug deeply into the sand roads. By measuring the distance between the tracks, Deerslayer could judge their size and speed. The tracks themselves told him better than any textbook when they had last passed. If the sand still slid into the track, it was recent. If the edges were rounded, it was a day old. If the track was smudged and unclear, it could be a week old. It all depended upon the weather. A good rain wiped them out in no time.

Deerslayer knew deer, but never . . . never this close. He figured they were yearlings, born the previous spring, and now on their own. He reached out and stroked the head of the nearest one. It shivered beneath his touch. The other one, half buried in the fallen branches of the pine tree, picked up its head and stared him down. Deerslayer edged closer. "So you want to be petted too. O.K.!" He smoothed his hand across the back of its neck. He sat close and laid its head on his lap. Its legs moved in slow motion, trying to get a grip on something. Weakly the deer butted him in the stomach.

"Good!" he laughed. "You've got some spunk left. You're going to need it." The reddish-brown fur on their backs was burned in spots. The smell of burned hair sickened Deerslayer. They both looked ragged.

"That's what I'll call you two: Raggedy Ann and Andy! No, make that just Ann and Andy." He hugged the spunky one close to his chest. "You're Andy!" Then patting the other's flank, "And you, my pretty, will be called Ann." Deerslayer shot a quick look at the sky through the overhead branches. "O.K.! I'll take care of them. Don't worry!" he yelled to Hiawatha, up there somewhere.

"The first thing we have to do is to get you some water." He rubbed their legs, which hardly moved. They could not rise. "O.K. I'll get it for you." He ran to the base of the hill, and cupped his hands in the clear stream. By the time he splashed some water over their heads, only drops remained.

"This will never do."

He grabbed the ax from the box. Selecting a fallen log,

39

he chopped a hollow in it. It held about a quart of water. He ran up and down the hill for an hour, soaking down the sick deer. They showed some signs of movement. He held the homemade bowl beneath their lips. Ann did not drink. Andy tried. Deerslayer dipped his fingers in the water. Andy sucked the liquid from his fingers. Deerslayer expected him to bite, but he did not. When Andy had his fill, his eyes cleared a little. Deerslayer turned to Ann, whose tongue still dangled from her mouth . . . wheezing. He cupped a handful of water into her open mouth. He heard the water wash down her throat. She did not swallow. Her fur was still matted from the bath.

That evening Deerslayer wrapped his arms about both heads, which rested on his chest. They felt warm and alive. That is all that matters, he thought. He felt refreshed. For years, someone had taken care of him. Now it was his turn and it felt good. For once something depended on him. A shrill whistling sound arose outside, but Deerslayer had already fallen asleep.

Through an umbrella of branches, the morning sun splashed over his closed eyelids like fat on a hot griddle. Without moving, he felt the heads on his chest. Both heaved up and down in a steady motion. Placing the heads carefully on the leafy pillows beside him, he rose and stretched outside the shelter of pine needles. It was a great day. He felt hungry, but that would have to wait.

Taking his bowl, he tore blades of grass into small pieces. He threw in some sassafras leaves for good measure. If the Indians used it for medicine, it just might work. He mixed some water into the soup, and crouched inside the shelter.

Andy tried to get up. He made it to a kneeling position. His eyes blinked when he saw Deerslayer. Ann still wheezed on the ground. Her ribs stood out beneath her tightly drawn skin. A film covered her half-closed eyes. Deerslayer held her head in both hands and cried. She looked so helpless, so pitiful. He looked deep into her eyes, wondering what was behind them. What was happening behind those deep pools? Did she understand? He shoved a fistful of grass into her mouth. It dribbled down the side. Andy was already dipping into the bowl—chomping away. He emptied it in no time.

Deerslayer mixed another batch of soup and set it before Andy. He dove right in, without so much as a thank you. As Andy ate, Deerslayer rubbed the deer behind the ears and stroked his back. Andy accepted the touching, but continued to eat.

Deerslayer stood on the top of the hill and looked eastward. The head fire was out. A few small brush fires still smoked in the distance. The blackened land would recover, he knew. The Pine Barrens was famous for that. In fact, fire speeded its growth. He headed into the burned land—now cool beneath his feet.

He explored the land. It was not dead. A loud *pop* exploded to his right. Looking down, he saw a pinecone shoot out tiny seeds in all directions. The cone from the pitch pine. It only opened after a fire. Deerslayer smiled. With fire came new life. Ashes fertilized the ground. Soon the seedlings would rise from the ashes. Shoots from the scrub oak, like snakes, will finger their way to sunlight through the black peat. Shrubs and ground cover will all

41

but erase the destruction. And life will continue in the Pines as it has for thousands of years.

Deerslayer picked up a dead rabbit, caught by the fire. Its hair was completely burned from its body. He cleaned it, and bit into the cooked flesh. It tasted good. The meat would remain edible for a few days at least. If he did not eat it, the turkey buzzards would. Even dead things had a purpose in the Pines. So that others might live.

With a full stomach, he returned to Ann and Andy. Their conditions remained the same. All day long, he wet the two deer down to lower their fevers. He tried force-feeding Ann, but she did not respond. Both deer slept most of the day. He dozed off himself a few times with the deer curled close to his side. The huge ball of orange sank through the pines just outside the shelter. The entire sun filled the entrance, shining so brightly that Deerslayer had to squint his eyes. Then he saw it. He blinked twice to be sure. Yes, it stood there in the entrance, its outline blurred by the burning sun behind it. A giant buck deer!

It did not move. It did not blink its eyes. From the neck down, its body disappeared in the encircling glow. Its awesome antlers—twelve pointed—just cleared the top of the entranceway. Its eyes glowed red—brighter than the sun.

Its nose and eyes were circled in white fur against a background of chestnut brown. The base of its ancient antlers, two feet long, was gnarled and brushed with black velvet. An ugly, two-inch scar curved across the bridge of its nose to a point just beneath its left eye. It was huge!

Deerslayer stared, openmouthed. Andy grunted, then

42

lifted himself to a standing position. His knees wobbled. Too stunned to move, Deerslayer watched the yearling stiffen his legs until he stood as firm as a pine tree. The red eyes of Big Buck glowed into Andy's eyes, giving him strength and courage.

Deerslayer looked back to the entranceway. Big Buck was gone. Instead, the half sun dipped past the horizon, like a giant envelope sliding down a maildrop, outside the shelter. Until it too was gone.

After a moment, Deerslayer spoke. "See, your dad has returned. He wants you guys to get better." A low rush of air behind him caused Deerslayer to twist around where he sat. Ann still lay there with her tongue hanging from her mouth. Her eyelids hung half open, without expression. Deerslayer felt for a pulse, a heartbeat . . . anything. Ann did not move. She would never move again. She was dead. Deerslayer threw his arms across the young doe's body. "Why do things have to die?" he yelled. *"Why?"*

As the evening shadows drifted into night, Deerslayer carried Ann to the burned-out section of woods. He closed her eyelids and tied her mouth shut with a twisted piece of cedar bark. She looked stately and regal, like a fallen princess. Kneeling over her in the darkening gloom, he raised his eyes to the few dots of starlight in the gray sky above him.

"If there is a deer heaven, take good care of her. We never really got to know each other, but we were good friends. Take care of Ann. Make sure she is happy." He turned to leave. He left her there on the ground, so that others might live.

Back at the shelter, Andy licked the bowl dry. He sank to his knees again, too weak to stand longer. Deerslayer finished the last of the rabbit, then sank his head into a bed of leaves. He listened to Andy's heavy breathing beside him. Outside, the whippoorwill sang its song, and a woodchuck rubbed the sleep from its eyes.

Deerslayer thought of the buck returning to its own kind. He did not really know if the buck was Andy's father. But it sounded better that way. He thought of Russ. He would have the whole police force out searching for him by now. Maybe even the National Guard. He pictured them all beating the bushes for a scared young boy. Deerslayer laughed. He saw Russ in the lead, with his potbelly and blue socks. Some woodsman! He'll never find me . . . never. Just before he drifted off to sleep, he wondered out loud, "Will Russ be looking for me at all?"

Next morning, after feeding Andy, Deerslayer gobbled down a breakfast of fresh blueberries and cedar water. He had a lot to do. First he coaxed the yearling from the shelter and led him beneath a tree. Andy looked spry this morning, taking in all the sights. With his ax, Deerslayer went to work on the inside of the shelter. He chopped away the branches until the interior was clear. He laid pine boughs on the floor. He searched the woods until he found a sour gum tree. It stood out, with its tall slender trunk and dark polished leaves. He chopped an armful of branches.

Carefully he wove the branches into the roof until it looked solid enough. He decided to leave the entrance clear for now. Maybe later he might make a door. In one corner, he set four oak trunks on the ground in the shape of a double bed. Within their framework, he crumbled scented pine needles. It was big enough for both Andy and him. He dragged his box inside and placed it deep in a dark corner.

In the center, the leafy shelter stood four feet high. Once inside, Deerslayer had to bend over. But since he expected to be outside most of the time, it did not bother him. It was just a place for sleeping and bad weather, like an Indian bark hut. Later he might cover the roof with cedar bark or deerskin. No, he thought, not deerskin. Cedar bark will have to do.

Outside, Andy struggled to his feet. Wobbly, but standing. He looked up at Deerslayer.

"Good boy! Now we're moving. Let's go." He rubbed the deer's head with both hands. He held up a large leaf of skunk cabbage. Andy made a grab. Deerslayer pulled back. Andy took a few careful steps forward, nibbling at the leaf with outstretched neck. "Good boy!" Andy butted his head into Deerslayer's side. Deerslayer butted back—a little too hard. Andy fell in a heap, giving Deerslayer the saddest look the boy had ever seen.

Well, almost the saddest. The saddest look that he had ever seen came from Aimee, his stepsister. About three weeks after their parents married, Robert got the first of many orders: "Why don't you go out and play with Aimee? Why don't you watch Aimee? Why don't you bring Aimee with you to the baseball game?" Enough to make you sick. Robert took her to the game that day. It was a choose-up game. He was usually picked last, but now he had Aimee.

Aimee was eight years old—a scrawny kid with the

neck of a weasel, sad eyes, and a big mouth. "Girls don't play in our games," he snapped.

"I can play."

"Look, kid, just sit and watch."

"Daddy says that you have to let me play."

"He's your daddy, little girl, not mine. I don't have to listen to him."

"He's your daddy, too. That's what he said."

"Don't believe everything you hear," Robert said.

Aimee tucked her T-shirt into her blue shorts. "But your mother is my mother . . . isn't she?" Aimee asked.

Robert shook his head. "No, she's not. She's my mother. Remember . . . your mother went bye-bye, little girl." That was the saddest look that Robert had ever seen. That look in Aimee's eyes after he had said it. He regretted saying it the second the words left his mouth. He kicked a clump of hard clay into dust. Behind him, the guys started playing without him. They did not really need a second right fielder.

Robert started to put his arm around Aimee, this strange, helpless creature at his feet. He pulled back. "I didn't mean that, kid. Of course, she's your mother."

She looked up, brushing away the tears. "You're lying!"

"Would I lie to you? Come on, I was just kidding. I just wanted to see what kind of sport you are, that's all."

Aimee hesitated, then smiled. A slow smile, uncertain but there. She looked strangely familiar, looking up at him with tears in her eyes. As though he had seen her once before . . . somewhere in his past.

5

THE shrill whistling sound caught Deerslayer's ear just as he threw another log on the fire. He turned. At the base of the hill, a sweet pepper bush parted in the breeze, its branches flapping back and forth like the arms of a rag doll. The head of the giant deer pushed through. Big Buck! The bush all but hid the deer from view. It stood over four feet high at the shoulders.

The yearling wobbled from the shelter and headed for the big deer. Big Buck lowered its head, swinging the deadly antlers through the air. Andy stopped, sniffed the air, then moved forward again. Big Buck snorted and again lowered its antlers. Andy got the message. Unafraid, the yearling munched a cluster of blueberries. His lower jaw moved back and forth as he ate. The next time he looked up, Big Buck was gone. The deer had just melted into the pines. Andy hopped in and around the spot where last the giant deer had stood. But Big Buck had vanished, silently. Besides, the berries tasted good.

Deerslayer scratched his head, then leaned back to admire his work. At least now it looked like a basket. He had soaked the fuzzy inner bark of the cedar in the creek all night to soften it. Hanging a stick from a branch, he twisted the soft fibers around it, and tied them off. He continued this until several strands hung straight down. He wove more bark back and forth through the strands. He repeated this weaving until the basket was deep enough, then he fastened the ends and bottom. He wove baskets all day long, stopping when he had completed four of them. Sleep came quickly that night, with Andy beside him.

The next day he lucked out. While washing in the creek, he caught a snapping turtle. Meat! He cut the white meat into chunks and threw them into one of the two coffee cans from the box. An hour of boiling should do it. While he waited for breakfast, he filled the baskets with blueberries. He set them on top of the hill to dry in the sun. He planned to store them underground, basket and all, for emergency food. He figured his only problem would be the birds. But Andy had other ideas. He was halfway through the first basket before Deerslayer shooed the deer away. Deerslayer set the baskets high in the forked branches of a pitch pine, where they still caught the sunlight.

Returning to his campfire, he tossed some onions into the stew. The first mouthfuls were hot . . . too hot to eat. He blew on the steaming mixture. It tasted just fine, almost like boiled chicken. With his knife, he scraped the turtle shell clean to be used later. Here in the middle of nowhere, a turtle shell was a treasure.

A 747 jet zoomed overhead, its shock waves vibrating the stew in the pot. Deerslayer watched it without regret. Civilization was so close to him, yet so far away. He wanted to keep it that way.

From the top of the hill, he surveyed his kingdom. To the east, the smoke had stopped. To the south, a green carpet of pitch pine stretched at his feet, broken in spots by lonely patches of white sand. Crows circled the distant spikes of cedar trees. The clouds floated so close that he felt he could just reach out and touch them. He had not noticed clouds much before, but now they looked majestic—twisting and changing into a thousand shapes. The blue sky stretched from horizon to horizon. Truly a place not of this earth, he thought.

A man's voice boomed behind him. "Turtle's not bad. Needs a touch more onion, though."

Enraged rather than scared, Deerslayer raced to the campfire, but stopped short at the sight of the man. He was six feet tall and as slim as a pine trunk. Leaning over the coffee can, he sucked the turtle stew from his fingers and smiled.

"Us woodsmen share our food, don't we?" His voice was soft, unlike the hardness of his face. Deerslayer could only nod. "Good," the man snapped, "now come and sit down."

Deerslayer hesitated.

"Come on!" the man said. "I won't bite you. And put some water up for tea. Nothing like snapping turtle and sassafras tea. Ummm!"

The man looked ancient to Deerslayer, his leathery skin wrinkled and folded from a thousand winters. His face was thin and angular, haloed by snow-white hair, which fell over his shoulders and down the front of his chest. He had no beard. He wore a loud sports shirt and Bermuda shorts, which came just below his bony knees. He wore leather sandals.

Deerslayer set the pot of water on the fire, and looked at the old man, who sat, cross-legged, opposite him. The boy was not frightened as he spoke. "Do you always take what you want from people?"

The old man paused in his munching. He had no teeth. "No! Just from the cooking fires of fools." Deerslayer reddened. "Only fools cook snapping turtles without salt."

"I have no salt!"

"Take mine then." The old man threw a Baggie full of salt on the ground next to Deerslayer. "By the way, what's your name?"

"Deerslayer!"

The man's eyes twinkled. "Deerslayer, huh? Kill many deer, have ya?"

"I do all right," Deerslayer lied.

"How d'ya go about it? Killing deer, that is. Do you shoot them? Or sneak up on them and stab them?"

"I get by," Deerslayer said.

"Oh, I know that. But how do you kill them? Throw pinecones at them, do ya? Or maybe train them to jump right into your cooking pot?"

Deerslayer shook his head. "I don't have to answer your dumb questions. And what's your name? I told you mine."

"Well, folks around call me the Deerman of the Pines.

Most call me mad. You can call me what you want. A man's name don't matter much. He's the same man whether you call him Charlie or mad or late for supper." The old man laughed at his own joke. Deerslayer did not get it.

"How did you find me?" Deerslayer asked.

"You leave a trail bigger than Route 9. I've been on to you for some days now."

Deerslayer offered the steaming tea to the old man, then poured some for himself. "I don't believe a word of it," he snapped.

The old man laughed. "Son, a slit throat is not a natural way of dying. Leastways not for a squirrel."

"You left that squirrel for me?"

"You looked hungry, boy. Us woodsmen have to stick together."

Deerslayer studied the features of the old man's face. It reminded him of Chief Sitting Bull. "Are you an Indian?"

"Right! I am the best Indian in the country. My great-great-grandfather was chief of the Delawares. Poor guy died of food poisoning at Indian Mills, eating a can of Boston beans. Poor guy should have stayed in the Pines like me."

Somehow Deerslayer was unconvinced. "Are you really an Indian?"

"Would I lie to you, boy? I've been out in these Barrens since I was knee-high to an ant. You can call me Deerman. It's an ancient Apache name."

"I thought you said you were from the Delaware tribe."

"Delaware! Apache! What's the difference? I come

51

from many tribes. Call me Many-Tribes, then . . . I don't mind." Leaning over, he gently pressed his fingers over Deerslayer's swollen shoulder. "I'll fix that up for you. Got some magic powder at my place."

Andy broke through the underbrush, walked up to Many-Tribes and licked his neck. The old man hardly noticed. He draped an arm around the deer's neck, then turned to Deerslayer. "You did a good job of fixing up the yearling, Deerkiller."

"Slayer! Deerslayer!"

"Oh, I'm sorry. I figured that a deerslayer kills deer, not fixes 'em up."

Deerslayer shifted uneasily on the ground. He had to change the subject. "Where do you come from?" he asked.

Many-Tribes stood up, banging his head against a low-hanging branch. He flicked it aside. "We don't talk about the past here. Besides, I didn't ask why you lost yourself out here."

"I'm not lost!" Deerslayer snapped. Imagine a woodsman being lost!

Many-Tribes held his arms in front of his face and laughed. "Boy, you are a touchy one, aren't you?" He tightened the belt on his shorts. "Now, let's go. It's about an hour's walk from here."

Deerslayer held back. "I don't think I want to go with you."

The old man shook his head. "Boy, you're something else. Look, I just figure that you like deer, despite your dumb name. You do like deer, don't you?"

Without looking up, Deerslayer managed a nod.

"Well, I want to show you why some folks call me Deerman. O.K.?"

Deerslayer rolled his arm around in its shoulder socket. It began to throb. "Well . . . O.K., I guess." He followed through the underbrush. The old man already five strides ahead of him. Andy followed close behind.

6

DEERSLAYER lost count of the number of creeks they crossed and the hills they climbed. The sun slid past noon, throwing small shadows to the east. The trail followed a sand road for half a mile, then cut sharply into the underbrush past a fallen oak tree. Many-Tribes did not pause. He crashed through the thick growth like a Sherman tank. Deerslayer had to run to keep up.

After a ways, the old man suddenly sank into a thick cedar forest. The tangled underbrush swallowed him from sight. Deerslayer followed, but lost the trail. For ten minutes he hacked his way through the bushes. Thorny branches clawed at his body. Twisted vines scraped against his throbbing shoulder. With his hunting knife, he took a wild swipe at a grapevine as thick as a marsh reed in full bloom. He missed, spun full circle, then tumbled into a clearing. It was the size of a football field. He gasped.

Deer grazed everywhere in the field. Fawns played between the legs of their mothers. Bucks lazily drank from a pond in the middle of the emerald clearing. None stood guard. "There must be over a hundred deer here," he whistled. A doe looked up from her grazing, frowned at the smelly intruder, then resumed eating. She stood four feet away.

A thick growth of cedars circled the field. Thornbushes plugged the base of the living wall, sealing off the outside world. One hidden deer run led to and from the encampment. A small cabin was in the center of the field near the pond. The old man waved from the doorway.

Deerslayer sank onto a wooden bench alongside the doorway. He was exhausted.

"Now that you're here, let me look at that burn," the old man said, pressing the shoulder. This time Deerslayer did not refuse. His shoulder ached from the bushes. He still wore only swim trunks. His upper body was scratched and bleeding in spots. Many-Tribes slipped inside the cabin.

He reappeared with a bowl in his hand. "Don't worry, it won't hurt none. It's just some dried sphagnum moss, soaked in the leaves of skunk cabbage. My great-grandfather of the Mohican tribe—up in New York State, you know—used it all the time for arrow wounds."

"Mohicans!" Deerslayer looked surprised. The old man laughed, bathing the wound. It felt cool and refreshing. Deerslayer almost closed his eyes.

"How do you keep all these deer here?" he asked, watching the animals. They looked so content and safe. Not uptight the way they did in the woods.

"Oh, they come and go as they please. No one can keep

'em anywhere they don't want to be. Except by *slaying* them, of course."

"O.K.!" Deerslayer snapped. "Will you lay off with that name, already!" He brushed some twigs from his chest. "And you live out here all alone?" The old man nodded and resoaked the moss. "What do you eat?" Deerslayer winced from the pain.

The old man did not look up. "Deer meat!"

Deerslayer frowned. "But you said . . . "

"Oh, I don't kill them," the old man laughed and set the bowl down. "I wouldn't kill any living thing. The deer come back here. When they're wounded by poachers or hunters, they return home. I fix 'em up. They trust me like family. But some don't make it and die—right in my arms. I don't bury them. Like the Indians, I use every part of their body. Bones, flesh, hides. In a way, they never leave this place. Even in death they stay here."

The old man rose. "Here, let me show you something."

Deerslayer followed him inside the cabin. He saw no furniture, just a pile of pine needles in a corner that served as a bed. It did have a fireplace of sandstone and mud. The logs of the walls were sealed with mud and straw. The old man lit a knob of pitch pine from the fire. The room danced in its glow. Its sweet smell filled every corner.

Many-Tribes ran his hand across one deerskin, a dark bronze in color. "This here's Mabel. Died a few summers back of a shotgun blast. She had seven fawns in all." He uncovered five more skins. "And here's Henry. He was some stubborn old buck, always bossing everyone around. Fought many a good fight, old Henry did. A real stubborn buck. Until one day he just gave up. He just lay down and died." The old man faced Deerslayer. "Don't ever give up, boy. You fight for whatever you want in life. You hear me, boy?"

Deerslayer nodded. "I know where you're coming from."

"What?"

"Never mind! I understand."

Many-Tribes ran his hands over the large pile of deer-skins. He choked up, turning his head away. "Yeah, old Henry just gave up. And that was the end of it."

Deerslayer shifted uneasily and wanted to get off the subject. "But the salt? Where do you get your salt?" he asked.

Many-Tribes ran the back of his hand across his eyes. "Oh, I go into town from time to time. To pick up my Social Security check at the post office and stock up on some vittles." He held up the skin from the buck named Henry, admiring it. "Look, boy, now that you're here, let me make you a coat or something. You can't go around these woods with nothing on top. You'll be cut to ribbons."

Deerslayer shook him off. "No, that's O.K."

The old man measured the boy's shoulders before he could stop him. Many-Tribes sliced a hole in the center of the hide with his hunting knife. He slipped it over Deerslayer's head like a poncho. It fell past his waist and weighed a ton. "There . . . perfect fit! You'll make old Henry happy."

Deerslayer said thanks. He did not want to offend the old man. A chill ran through his body despite the heavy warmth of his new cape. Maybe this old guy really is mad, he thought.

"Sally!" Many-Tribes yelled. Then over his shoulder to Deerslayer, "This you've got to see." From a group of six deer, one perky doe pranced toward the cabin. She walked with a slight limp and rubbed her flank against the old man like a cat against a chair leg.

"Take a look at her leg," Many-Tribes said. Squatting down, Deerslayer ran his hand along the deer's leg, but saw nothing.

"Here! Look here!" The old man held back some fur, revealing three round scars, each the size of a silver dollar. "Some hunter used dumdum bullets on her. They file down the point of the shell. It doesn't pierce the skin; it shatters it. But we fixed her up. With moss and skunk cabbage. Same stuff I used on you."

Deerslayer gave a low whistle. "That's neat work. You should have been a veterinarian. Did you ever think of going back to the city? You'd make a lot of money as a vet."

Many-Tribes pulled an apple from his pocket and held it out for Sally. She nibbled at it in his hand.

"Money?" he snorted. "I make more money here than the richest man in the world. You tell me—now listen close—if I gave you a thousand . . . no, a million dollars, could you go out and buy ten pounds of sunshine? They don't sell that at the Grand Union. I'm serious now."

Deerslayer shook his head. The old man had made his point.

"Could you buy a half pound of happiness, or two quarts of fresh air?" Many-Tribes breathed in a gulpful of cedar air. "Of course, you couldn't. You can't buy the

58

important things. They're free. Men buy one car, then two, then they need three. Another TV set. Another stereo. They're never happy that way. Any time you buy something, it buys you. Because you *need* it. If you don't need it, you're O.K. But this"—he swept his arm across the clearing and toward the sky—"this is free. This is where it's at."

Deerslayer followed the sweep of his arm. The field looked like a scene from a picture book—the deer contentedly grazing, the sun just dipping below the treetops to his right. "And there is peace in the world; and he is happy."

"Whatya say?" Many-Tribes asked.

"Oh, nothing," Deerslayer said. "Just a passing thought. By the way, where did you get the apple?"

"Years ago, some Italian prince built a mansion down a ways. He planted a whole apple orchard. Not one brick of the old three-story mansion is left, but the apple trees still blossom every year. That should tell you something."

Deerslayer stretched his legs. The old man chewed a stalk of grass with his gums. He gave Deerslayer a long look before talking. "I know, you want to get moving. Got to get away. Got to keep running. I understand."

"I should get back before nightfall. Andy—he's the yearling—did not make it through that thicket. He'll be wondering about me," Deerslayer said.

"Just remember that I'm here. Anytime you want some company, just yell."

Deerslayer turned to leave, then stopped short. "There's one more thing I've been meaning to ask you. Where's Big Buck?"

"Who?"

"Big Buck!" Deerslayer quickly described the giant deer. "A twelve-pointer!"

The old man shook his head. "I ain't seen any sign of no twelve-pointer with a scar like that. And I know every buck, doe, and fawn this side of Cape May. No, I think you're seeing things."

"No, I saw him all right. Saw him with my own eyes."

Many-Tribes shook his head. "Ain't no such animal, boy. Never was, and never will be. I'd know about it if there was."

Deerslayer dropped it. No sense arguing with a brick wall, he thought. Waving good-by, he cut through the thicket the way he had come. He took a last look behind him. The deer looked up from their grazing, shivered their flanks, then returned to their food. The trip back seemed faster. He arrived home just after sunset. He saw no sign of Andy along the way.

About midnight, he heard a loud growling outside the entrance of his shelter. On hands and knees, he strained his eyes into the blackness of the moonless night. Eight pairs of eyes stared back at him. The eyes returned to haunt him, as the blood in his veins turned to ice.

7

IN the blackness of the night, the eyes glowed red, reflecting the few glowing embers of the campfire. They moved closer. Deerslayer backed up in his small shelter on all fours until he could back up no farther. The eyes sensed his fear. They did not bob up and down when they moved. They floated above the ground like pinpoints of light, heading toward him.

The low growl of the lead animal, a scrawny police dog, broke the silence. Wild dogs! Deerslayer had heard of them, but had passed them off as scare stories to keep little kids out of the woods. Now they proved real enough. The eyes belonged to a pack of strays, about sixteen of them. Their ribs stood out like the spokes of an umbrella; patches of fur were missing in spots. Between growls, their tongues dangled from the corners of their mouths. They looked mean and hungry.

Some were runaways like himself, drooling for a meal. After being chased from the town garbage pails, they had fled into the Pines. There was no place else to go. Some had been abandoned by tourists—left behind when the vacation ended. All were mean and hungry.

Pet dogs are not wild, Deerslayer tried to convince himself. They were only tame animals living in the wilds like himself. But they had forgotten how to live off the land. Years of flea collars and Gravy Train had made them soft. They had forgotten their past. They had lost the swiftness of the deer, the cunning of the fox, and the meanness of the weasel.

But they fought to survive. Something in their animal brains told them to kill or be killed. Some dim spark from their ancient past, long since buried, urged them on. To hunt, to eat any meal that came their way. Right now their meal was Deerslayer, and he knew it.

Breathing heavily, he tore a hole in the roof of his shelter. Parting the overhead branches, he pulled himself up. The dogs shuffled below. The roof was not solid enough to hold his weight. It sagged for one breathless moment, then stopped. A large branch forked from the main trunk of the fallen tree, just clearing the roof. Higher up, it snagged in the fork of a living pine. Deerslayer wrapped both arms and legs around the branch, like a monkey on a pole, and pulled himself up.

He grabbed a branch for support, but it snapped in his grasp. In the blackness, unseen fingers of wood clawed his face. He looked up to where the branch met the nearby pine. It balanced ever so slightly within the fork. Hold me, he prayed. His heart pounded wildly.

Not another asthma attack! he panicked. Not now! He strained to fight it off. On the branch halfway between the roof and the fork in the tree, he rested. In the darkness, he barely made out the shapes of the dogs below. Their eyes glowed red.

But he heard their growling. Not a bark, nor a yelp. A low, gurgling sound from deep within their throats. They then exploded around the campsite in their excitement. They tore everything apart in search of food. One chewed the coffee can once filled with turtle soup. It sank its teeth through the metal like a hot knife through butter.

One mongrel sniffed the chunk of turtle meat which had fallen into the bed of glowing embers. It turned the meat over with its nose and bit in. The embers sizzled its nose. A wild yelp rang out. The dog ran in pain, slamming into the other dogs, who nipped at its legs and flank. The large police dog jumped the mongrel from the rear, landing on its back. He sank his teeth into the burned dog's neck until it stopped yelping. The police dog wandered back to his spot beneath the tree. He knew where his prey was going. He would wait for it.

Satisfied that they had cleared the area of food, the pack settled down for the night on empty stomachs. Their main course still shook in the tree above them. Maybe he would come down. A cocker spaniel, covered with burrs, circled one spot on the ground twenty times before flopping over, as it had done a hundred nights on a rug before a fireplace in another lifetime somewhere. The night turned still. A few tree frogs croaked in the distance.

From the north, a gentle breeze tickled the pine needles and blew through Deerslayer's curly hair. Tightly he held the branch, as the bark dug deep gashes into his cheek. Below, the growling had stopped—only a whimper arose now and then in the dogs' troubled sleep. Deerslayer made his move upward, holding his breath. If only this branch holds, he prayed. Hand over hand, foot over foot, he inched higher. The living pine was inches away. Already its needles brushed his face. He knew that the branch was too thin to support his weight this high up. He would have to jump for it. Sucking in a huge gulp of air, he lunged. His body crashed against the tree trunk, his arms and legs encircling it in one movement. His breath came short and fast.

On the ground below, the pack went wild. They barked and yelped themselves into a frenzy. Each wanted to be the first to leap upon the food from the sky. Deerslayer remained still, feeling a warm glow inside. Funny! It was the thrill of the hunt, even though he was on the wrong side. It was fear for his life. It was survival! At the base of the tree, the big police dog looked up into the overhead branches. He did not bark or carry on like the other dogs. His mouth rippled in a low growl, baring his sharp teeth. He waited.

The sun peeked over the green meadow to the east. Deerslayer's eyes were puffy from the sleepless night. He opened and closed his mouth; it tasted dry. He was hungry and thirsty, but in one piece. The dogs began their prowl beneath the tree. One by one they stalked in a wide circle, as if ordered. The police dog sneered upward. In the center of the pack, he held his post. Almost unconcerned, yet alert, like a lifeguard on a beachful of fun seekers. The other dogs paid little attention to the police dog, but they knew he was watching them—watching.

For the first time in his life, Deerslayer felt the horror of survival. He felt what the squirrel felt before the stick struck it down. He felt what the bullfrog felt before the last blow. He felt what all animals feel when the end is near. He shivered.

Andy! he thought. Where is that deer? He searched the area, but saw no signs of him. "Stay away, boy," he whispered. I must be flipping out, he thought. Here I am in danger for my *life,* and I think about a crummy deer. Boy!

The morning came and went. When the sun slipped two hands past noon, the dogs grew restless. They whimpered, and looked at the lead dog from the corners of their eyes. He did not move. Deerslayer figured that they would be gone by now. They must be starving to hang around this long. He had to do something. He looked at the campfire below. A few sparks of red still glowed in the ashes.

Deerslayer cracked one of the many dead branches from the trunk. He threw it at the dogs. The cocker spaniel yelped and flew beneath a bush. The police dog laughed—or at least it looked that way. The dog did not budge.

"He's a mean one," Deerslayer moaned. He threw more sticks, but they did nothing at all, except scare the sickly, little cocker spaniel. He tried a different move. A desperate plan that just might work. But he had to get to the box in the shelter.

He secured the fallen pine branch as best he could within the fork of the tree. He crawled down the branch backward. It was too small, about the thickness of two fingers, but he had to try. He wiggled his legs. The branch shuddered, then snapped. Still clutching the branch, he fell down. The dogs exploded on the ground below him. Foam drooled from their mouths.

Six feet above the ground, the branch sprang back like a rubber band, shivered a few times, then hung limply like a dead fish.

Deerslayer dangled upside down. The dogs leaped for his face. The police dog moved in, as the others moved aside. Deerslayer turned himself around and clawed at the broken branch. The police dog leaped, snapping his teeth inches from Deerslayer's feet. He felt its hot breath across his toes. He finally reached the main branch and held fast. That was too close!

He rested. He decided to go through with his original plan. I can't stay up here another night, he reasoned. Softly he planted his feet on the roof of his shelter. He still held the branch to be sure that the roof did not cave in. He parted the woven roof and looked inside. Most of the dogs were outside, prowling in the nearby woods. Only the cocker spaniel was curled up in Deerslayer's bed. It looked so soft and cute. The box was directly behind him. Silently Deerslayer dropped to the ground, then froze.

A few dogs bayed in the distance. The cocker awoke, and tilted its head to one side, studying Deerslayer.

"Shhhh! Nice boy," he soothed. "Don't bark. You don't want to give me away, do you?" The cocker looked puzzled. This two-legged creature looked familiar, not dangerous. It held back its growl for now.

"Good boy," Deerslayer whispered. He patted its

head, looking over his shoulder at the entrance. He grabbed the shotgun cartridges from inside the box. Just as he climbed through the hole in the roof, a Doberman pinscher dashed through the entrance.

Securing a foothold on the branch, Deerslayer tossed a cartridge into the fireplace. Missed! The second try landed true. And the third! That was enough. The hot coals ignited the gunpowder in the cartridges. The first blast rocked the woods. The second exploded ten seconds after. The dogs scattered out of sight. Deerslayer waited a few minutes before jumping down.

He tore some dandelions from the ground, shoving the leaves into his mouth. Running down the hill, he dove into a patch of raspberries. The berries were black and plump. Soon his mouth dripped with the juices. Once satisfied, he plunged his head into the cool creek water. He swallowed long and hard. He felt its refreshing coolness flow down his throat.

Many-Tribes was right, he thought. You can't buy this for a million dollars.

Looking over the campsite, he groaned. "What a mess!" As he reset the sandstones around his fireplace, he heard a sad bleating, like a calf in pain.

"Andy!" He ran into the woods. Off to his right, he spotted movement in the bushes. The undergrowth was so thick that he could only see ten feet ahead of him.

"Andy!" he yelled. The rustling headed east, and Deerslayer followed.

At one of the many sand roads that crossed his trail, Andy paused, twisting his head over his shoulder. He had a sad, frightened look in his eyes.

"It's me, Andy!" Deerslayer yelled. "Don't you recognize me?"

The yearling crashed ahead on the run.

Those dogs must have scared him out of his senses, Deerslayer figured. He followed the pounding hooves.

The chase took him over a hill and into the burned woods. Wintergreen and Virginia creeper already covered the blackened ground. Red tips blossomed within the devil's matches lichen. From a distance the spots looked like drops of blood. The burned tree trunks looked like gnarled fingers, begging for mercy. Many trees had escaped the fire. Especially the scrub oak and jack pine. In spots the crown fire had completely missed the bottom cover of sumac and shadbush. A heavy smell of charcoal hung in the air. Deerslayer snapped a wintergreen leaf in his mouth. It tasted sharp and refreshing.

An hour later the chase ended. Andy rested in a small hollow, eating. Deerslayer approached slowly.

"Steady, boy . . . steady."

Andy did not move. He seemed to recognize Deerslayer, and let the boy pet him.

"So you came to your senses at last," Deerslayer smiled. Andy rubbed his head beneath Deerslayer's arm. Falling on the ground, Deerslayer rubbed his fingers over his eyes until they hurt.

"Now, I get a headache," he moaned. His stomach growled in hunger. Meat hunger!

"Let's see! That Piney shack is around here someplace. Maybe they'll give me some food." Andy did not pause in his grazing. "Well, asking for help is not all that bad, you

68

know," Deerslayer snapped. "Didn't the old man say that us woodsmen have to help each other out? I mean, someone helps you, and you help him back. That's how it works, Andy. You have to learn that to survive."

Deerslayer felt a heavy weight rise from his body as he spoke. Somehow he felt differently toward people now. He was not afraid to ask for help—to even admit that he might need help. Everyone needs help sometimes.

He searched the woods for ten minutes before he saw the faint outline of the shack in a clump of oaks and red maples. Remembering the dogs, he approached the house slowly. He had no idea where the dogs were, or even if they might not be watching him right now. He pictured the lead dog sailing through the air with foam trailing from his mouth. He quickened his step.

The cabin squatted close to the ground like a toadstool. The fire had completely passed over it. There was a strange silence about the place. The area looked lived in all right. No cobwebs around the door or windows. Beaten earth on the path. Deerslayer knocked on the door. No reply! He knocked again. Still getting no answer, he pushed open the door and looked inside. The air smelled musty and stale, like a tomb. Simple furniture cluttered the dirt floor. In the corner stood a cedar bed, covered with a yellowing bed sheet. Beneath it, in the dim light, a human form took shape. The form did not move.

"Excuse me!" Deerslayer gulped, turning away. "But I'm hungry. Been out in these woods too long, I guess." The form remained still. A yellow jacket buzzed from the ceiling, circled Deerslayer, then returned to its nest.

Deerslayer walked closer. "I really would appreciate some food. Anything you have!" Beneath the sheet, Deerslayer made out the outline of a person . . . a very thin person. It still did not move. "I hate being a pest, but . . ."

Deerslayer pulled away the sheet.

8

A SKELETON lay on the bed, its skull turned to one side. Its lower jaw gaped open; its hollow eye sockets stared emptily at the far wall. A spider wove a fragile web within its rib cage.

Deerslayer screamed. He ran a half mile down the road before the spider resumed its spinning.

Later, in his shelter with Andy, Deerslayer kept yelling over and over, "Don't ask questions! Don't ask questions! That skeleton's been there for years. Don't ask questions!" He did not. His hunger helped him to forget.

The waters from the slow-moving current of the creek backed up in a hollow, forming a large year-round marsh. It sparkled in the sunlight. Tall marsh grass lined its borders. It had no clear shoreline; the ground just became wetter and the water, deeper. The spikes of tall white cedars rose in the sluggish mire like sentinels. Some dead, twisted branches held an osprey nest.

The marsh contained many small ponds, backwaters, and bush clusters—ideal for wildlife. On its surface

71

floated white water lilies and blue flag iris, while pickerelweed fringed its edges. A white heron, standing on one leg, speared its dinner in the bottom mud. Nervous sandpipers skittered back and forth along the mudbanks. Deerslayer headed for the clump of cattail rushes.

Dark-brown cattails bobbed in the sea of spiked reeds. A few had already turned to seed, sending a snow cloud of fuzz into the air when disturbed. Large mounds of yellow salt hay covered the soggy soil beneath Deerslayer's feet. He followed the deep honks of the bullfrogs. They sat on sunken logs in the marsh. Some floated offshore, their two eye mounds just breaking the water's surface . . . watching.

Deerslayer dove for a log with outstretched arms. He missed and landed, nose deep, in the slime. He slid for two feet without stopping.

He sat up, covered with mud, and laughed. What a mess! He crawled back to a good covering of marsh reeds and waited for the bullfrogs to return. It seemed like hours, but they did return.

A snowy egret slowly drifted across the swamp, but Deerslayer hardly noticed. He jumped again, this time burying three croakers beneath his body. He waded through the arrowheads, which flourished near the shore. He felt for their tubers with his toes in the mud. He pulled up five roots of the plant and carried his meal back to camp.

He set a can of water on the fire and threw in the frogs' legs. His mouth watered. He peeled back the roots of the arrowhead plant and roasted them in the hot coals. He had read that they tasted like white potatoes. Having some free time, he rewove his shelter with saplings. He muttered a silent thanks to the branch that had supported him during the dog attack.

After his meal, he walked to a stand of cedars on the downhill slope of the rise. With his knife he cut a straight line through the bark from as high as he could reach to ground level. He then cut around the tree at both the highest and lowest points of the first cut. Carefully he peeled off the outer bark of the cedar. After stripping five trees this way, he gathered up the bark in both arms, and placed it underwater in the creek. He placed river stones over it to keep it from floating. After a week, the bark would become soft. Overlapped like shingles, it would go on the roof to keep out the rain.

With a full meal beneath his belt and some work completed, he leaned against a tree and dozed off. The thought of the grinning skeleton came to him. Skeletons used to remind him of Halloween and witches. But he had grown a little older these past weeks, a little wiser. Now skeletons reminded him of death.

His mother's bleeding face forced its way into his mind. It all returned like a tidal wave of twisted metal. Half dazed, he heard Aimee whimpering in the backseat and Russ cursing in the front. He tried to fight back the thoughts, but they proved too strong. Something inside his brain kept taunting him like a red-hot drill. How did it sound? What did his mother look like? He remembered the sickening crunch, the screaming tires, and the breaking glass. And his mother's dangling body!

It hung halfway out of the car. Her head lay in a pool of

73

blood on the asphalt. She did not move. She did not speak.

"Mom!" he yelled beneath the pine trees. But she did not answer him. He stood up.

Have to keep moving! Have to keep busy, he told himself. What to do? He decided to pay a call on Many-Tribes. Why not? It was still early enough. He plunged into the undergrowth. This time Andy did not follow.

He first heard it off to his right as he watched a king snake slither beneath a fallen log. A whistle! A policeman's whistle, followed by muffled voices. Russ *did* call the police! They were looking for *him*, right now. The footsteps came closer. Deerslayer dove into the marsh reeds and lay in knee-high water.

A group of four men stopped at the water's edge. One lit a cigarette, flipping the match toward Deerslayer. He wore a deputy sheriff's badge. The others looked like volunteer firemen. Russ was not among them.

"Doubt if the kid would of went into the marsh. He's scared, but not stupid."

The sheriff nodded. "I think you're right, Max. Let's go back and see if we can pick up his trail. It's gotta be here someplace." The four men retraced their steps.

"Scott! Do you hear me?" they yelled. "Scott!"

Deerslayer waited until the sound of the footsteps disappeared before he rose from the swamp. He brushed off the marsh grass. The bottom mud held him fast. He strained at his legs. Finally he pulled a foot free with a loud sucking sound. He stumbled onto shore and considered the problem. They must be looking for a lost

74

kid other than himself. People do wander into the Pine Barrens every year and get lost. Especially kids. They just wander away from their parents at some company picnic, never to be heard from again. Maybe that skeleton was some poor lost soul. Who knows?

He searched the banks for a trail. If he were lost, he would certainly stop for a drink. What do those guys know? Halfway around the swamp, he spotted a shallow depression from a child's sneaker. The water already rose within the track. The trail led to the water's edge. Two deep imprints in the mud looked like marks of the kid's knees as he knelt to drink. The footprints then turned into the woods. Deerslayer followed them.

The signs were unmistakable. Broken twigs, kicked-up leaves. Whoever had left this track had not tried to hide it. At one point the trail went full circle, only to return to the same spot. Like the trail of some scared kid. From the broken branches, Deerslayer figured the kid was about four feet tall, maybe eight years old. He picked up the plastic leg of a plastic doll. It looked like a Superman doll.

"The kid is probably holding the rest of it somewhere up ahead." Deerslayer pressed on, eating while he tracked. Night fell quickly. He could not see the trail ahead.

"Scott!" he yelled. He did not expect an answer. Moving off the trail, he buried himself in the leaves. He dreamed of Superman and skeletons.

The next morning Deerslayer arose before the sun. He picked up the trail, which now wandered west. "Hope those dogs aren't around," he moaned, "for the kid's sake." Deerslayer studied the broken vines of a raspberry patch. Mashed berries clearly marked the kid's footprint. He wore Keds sneakers, much smaller than his own.

Deerslayer topped a small rise and lost the trail. He grew frantic and circled back.

There, propped against a tree, a small body curled inside the twisting roots of a red maple . . . fast asleep. Deerslayer heaved a sigh of relief. He shook the boy by the shoulders.

"Hey! Wake up! You're O.K."

The boy opened his eyes, but his eyelids still covered half his eyes. He had a large nose and rubbery lips that danced in a baby's smile. A few scratches cut his face. His eyes twinkled.

"Hey, are you all right?" Deerslayer asked. The boy did not answer. "Are you O.K.?" Deerslayer asked again, but the boy did not respond. Deerslayer had thought as much. The boy was retarded. The red juice of the raspberries still stained his mouth. "O.K., then. I'll take care of you." Deerslayer felt his arms and legs for any broken bones. No, he was in top shape. He did not even look scared. Does he know what scared is? Deerslayer wondered. He pulled the boy to his feet and shoved the Superman doll into his hands. Scott smiled.

"Come on, we've got to get you back to your folks." Dark clouds rolled in from the coast. Swirling black masses did a dance above their heads. In the distance he heard the whistles. He stopped as the men drew near. He sat the boy in the middle of a small patch of clover. Scott looked happy enough just to sit there. He must be tired, Deerslayer thought. Scott threw the doll up and down.

Cupping his hands over his mouth, Deerslayer yelled, "I'm here! Over here! Help!" Then he ran into the woods.

The men discovered the boy just as the first drops of rain fell upon the ground. From his lookout, Deerslayer watched. One man, probably Scott's father, gathered up the boy in both arms, his tears falling as freely as the rain. "It's a miracle . . . a miracle!"

The miracle slid down the pitch pine and smiled. He felt good inside. The rain fell in buckets now, plowing into the sand and soaking the leaves. Deerslayer scampered beneath the shiny leaves of a swamp azalea bush. it was dry inside. Over an hour passed before the storm let up. The Pine Barrens dripped.

Deerslayer had no idea where he was. In his haste to follow the boy, he had not marked any trail. It was all new territory to him, even though it looked the same as any place else. The same stunted pines! The same scrub oaks! The same ferns growing in the lowlands! He could understand how some people got lost. Deerslayer returned to the trail. But it was gone. The rain had wiped it clean, like an eraser across a greenboard. He grew anxious. He circled the area three times, but still no trail. Deerslayer was lost.

Sure he could survive. Sure he could live off the land, but something inside urged him back to his own shelter. To his own campfire. To Andy. Back to something familiar. He even missed the dogs. At least they were something he knew, something he remembered. But *lost?*

Deerslayer roamed the countryside most of that day. The dampness from the recent storm bit into his bones.

Everything dripped. Each disturbed branch caused a flood over him. He passed the gutted remains of a moonshiner's still. Inside the twisted copper shell, he saw two spotted salamanders playing tag. He passed the cinder foundations of homes, now overgrown with moss. He passed the broken remains of chimneys. He passed the long depression of a cranberry bog. Growers dug out a large hollow, mostly by hand, then planted it with cranberry bushes. At harvesttime, the pickers would flood the field. Wading in the water, they would shake the submerged bushes. The berries, once free, would float to the surface, making an easy harvest.

Deerslayer could not believe that people like himself once walked here, once lived here, beneath these pines. Years ago! They were born, lived, and probably died right here in the Barrens. Without ever seeing a town, without ever leaving their sand roads. Years ago! Maybe centuries ago! Right on the spot where he now stood. Deerslayer shook his head.

Kids like himself, he thought. With mothers and fathers. Sure, they had their arguments. Deerslayer wondered what kids did on Saturdays, when every day was Saturday. And school? Did they have schools back here? And their fathers, he thought. Did they drink? Did they beat their kids? Were they thieves or moonshiners?

Whole generations lived and died here in the Pines. They lived with nature, season by season like the plants. Cranberries in the fall. Gathering moss for big-city florists, or pinecones for Christmas. Pineballers got four dollars per thousand cones, Deerslayer had once read. They picked and sold laurel stems. Anything for a dollar.

They made cedar tables, cedar chairs, and cedar shakes for houses. They sold firewood, and box turtles. Always with the season. And in the summer, they searched the hidden places for rare wild flowers and sold them to big-city collectors—wild magnolia, trailing arbutus, lady's slipper, and over twenty-three different kinds of orchid. They led experts to the rare curly grass fern, or to that unique tree frog that has suction cups for feet.

Deerslayer found it hard to believe. He sat in the middle of someone's home . . . someone's whole life . . . and he was *lost*. He felt more embarrassed than scared.

9

THE white-streaked chipmunk ran under Deerslayer's upraised knee, and dove into the grass. It popped up ten yards away, looked about nervously, then plunged into the thicket. That is when Deerslayer saw the antlers.

The big deer stood motionless within the thicket, his blue-black eyes shining, staring at Deerslayer.

"Big Buck!" he yelled. He ran to the deer. Big Buck bolted.

Through bushes and thickets, over hill and through hollow, Deerslayer followed the deer. Each time Deerslayer stopped, Big Buck stopped, keeping a good fifty yards between them. Deerslayer lost all track of time and place.

Two hours later, exhausted, Deerslayer fell to the ground. The area looked familiar. On all fours, he sucked in air. Andy licked the side of his face. He opened his eyes. Taken back, he saw that he was kneeling on the edge of his campsite. He pressed Andy close to his chest.

"I'm home, boy. Did you miss me?"

He searched the surrounding woods for sign of the big deer, but he had vanished. Deerslayer figured as much.

"Many-Tribes said that you don't exist," he yelled to the woods. "But I saw you." He fell asleep right there on the ground. Andy whimpered beside him.

The next morning Deerslayer awoke to find Andy eating the roof.

"O.K., boy," he laughed. "We'll fix that roof today."

He split more cedar bark and soaked it in water. The job took two days. When the bark felt rubbery, like smooth leather, he carried it from the creek and attached it to the roof with rope of inner bark. He stitched one strip low, then shingled the next strip overlapping the first. In a week he had completed the roof.

Deerslayer felt good. He had not had an asthma attack for a week. He pushed it from his mind.

"That chipmunk had the right idea about storing his food." Deerslayer used the next three days to gather his own food. "Can't live on a diet of berries," he thought out loud.

He made five more baskets and filled them with berries. He used the gum of the pitch pine to make the baskets waterproof. After drying the berries in the sun, he buried them, basket and all. He made a box of sticks, tying the sticks together with strips of deer hide from the cape that Many-Tribes had made for him. It was too big anyway. Propping up the box with a stick, he placed acorns and salt beneath the trap. He rigged a trip wire, so that when an animal grabbed the bait, the box would fall over him.

Before long, he had a steady supply of squirrels and

rabbits. He silently thanked the animals for their meat. Some he smoked over the fire; some he dried in the sun in long strips.

From a long cedar pole with a Y at one end, he made a net. Within the fork of the Y, he wove vines. Catching frogs was much easier now. He caught box turtles and snapping turtles. He caught salamanders, but decided not to eat them. He might in a pinch. He gathered mushrooms and stored them high in his shelter, both the beefsteak kind and the giant puffball. The edible morel with its white underbelly, tasted best fresh, even though it chewed like leather.

Each night before the sun sank in the west, he read his books, especially *Living off the Land*. It proved to be a big help in his search for food. He gathered acorns that had fallen last autumn and ground them between two slabs of sandstone. He mixed the flour with water for pancakes. To cut the bitter taste, he sprinkled blueberries, sometimes huckleberries, into the flour. He made it a point to return to that cranberry bog and harvest some for winter.

Many-Tribes visited a few times, checking up on his deer. At least that's the excuse he gave. He amazed Deerslayer with his knowledge of the Pines. He knew every bush, every plant and its use. He knew more than the books. Deerslayer hated to see him leave, but he understood. He did not press the old man.

Deerslayer gathered young fern stalks, not over six inches high. The older stalks were too tough to eat. After rubbing the fuzz from the tender greens, he boiled them in salt water. He tried pokeweed, sorrel, and watercress.

Before long, he was well stocked with smoked meat and greens. He dug the cattail root, although he preferred the arrowhead. All roots tasted bitter and had to be constantly boiled in at least three changes of water. Bitterroot was good, but hard to find. And, of course, he laid in a good supply of sassafras root for tea. Its sweet taste needed no sugar. Once he found some honey from a beehive, but the hives were few and far between. He crossed off sugar as a food.

In the creek and nearby marsh, Deerslayer fished for catfish and pickerel. The catfish tasted great, but the pickerel left a lot to be desired. It was all bone and muscle. Great sport, though. Deerslayer made sure that he fished at least once a week. Each day blended into the next as he checked his traps and prepared his harvest of wild plants.

But something was missing. Andy was good company, but now the deer grew restless. His daily trips into the wild took longer. Probably he was meeting his friends somewhere in the pines. Deerslayer watched a canvas-back duck with its mate fly low over the finger branches of cedar. Everything had someone; everything seemed to belong to something or someone. Deerslayer felt alone.

One evening, after a full meal of rabbit stew and watercress, Deerslayer read *Living off the Land* for the tenth time. He knew it by heart. Storm clouds covered the pines with a thick blanket of black. Night rolled in quickly. Raindrops the size of pinecones forced Deerslayer inside and drowned his campfire. He planned to build an indoor fireplace, but fire still scared him. A flying spark! A wayward breeze to fan the flames! The forest fire was too fresh in his mind for that now. He would figure out something in the future.

Lightning cracked to his right—a distant flash of light, then the slow roll of thunder. At home, he would have closed the shades and watched the static on the television screen. But here he sat in the middle of the storm. The lightning cracked closer. This time he heard a tree crash to the ground, pulling vines and blueberries with it. Andy huddled in the corner.

A weak smile crossed Deerslayer's face. "If we want to be part of nature, old buddy, we have to take the good with the bad." Another bolt of lightning cut him short. It struck just outside. Deerslayer smelled burning pine and stiffened. The rain blew sideways over the ground like a waving gray sheet, twisting in the wind. The howling grew louder.

Crash! Another bolt of lightning. This time the flash and the sound came together. It was right on top of him. He looked into the sky. "Where are you, Hiawatha? Protect your son." Instead of peace, another bolt of lightning crackled through the underbrush. Deerslayer hugged the shaking deer. "It'll be all right. Wait and see."

The thunder rolled over the shelter and sped northward. The rain still fell, but now it fell straight down. The worst was over. Deerslayer slipped into his cape and surveyed the damage ouside. A pine at the bottom of the hill still smoked, but no flames. The danger had passed.

The next day Deerslayer reset his traps. The storm had all but wrecked them. He had to make two new ones. Then he checked his baskets of stored food. One was waterlogged—probably a squirrel had ripped off its cover. The berries were ruined. The creek overflowed its bank. His favorite fishing spot floated six inches underwater.

The cedar roof had held back most of the downpour. He repaired the few cracks with pine gum, which kept falling out. It would be an endless job.

"This is getting to be too much like work," he mumbled.

One day, as Deerslayer split some logs, Andy limped into camp. A metal spring trap, long since illegal, bit into his right leg just above the hoof. The blood had already caked. Deerslayer tugged at the trap's jaws with no luck. He shoved a thick stick in between the ugly teeth and heaved, pulling out Andy's leg in one motion. The leg felt broken, Deerslayer feared that the rust from the trap might cause infection. He checked his books, but there was nothing in them for broken legs. He lifted Andy over his shoulder, grabbed both front legs with his hands, and headed for Many-Tribes. The old man would know what to do, if they could get there in time.

Deerslayer stopped many times along the way. "You're getting fat, Andy," he snapped past his ear. "Getting set for the winter?" Andy looked back with his large dumb eyes.

Deerslayer circled the wall this time, instead of breaking through the thick underbrush. He found the deer run. It was smaller than most. Branches parted, then fell back behind him to cover the entrance. He almost ran for the cabin. Out front Many-Tribes whittled a flute from a length of oak.

"You've got to help him, Many-Tribes!" Deerslayer begged. Gently he eased Andy onto the ground. His shoulders hurt.

Many-Tribes did not speak. Running a wrinkled hand over the deer's leg, he grunted. "It's broken all right, but no problem. My great-grandfather from the Seminole tribe in Florida taught me all there is to know about mending bones."

Deerslayer started to speak, but held back. It would wait until after Many-Tribes set the bone.

Many-Tribes spread his magic powder on the leg, then stuffed sphagnum moss over the wound. He bound it with a strip of deer hide. Laying two splints, one on each side, Many-Tribes tied them off. "That should do it. Now only nature can heal him." Many-Tribes resumed his carving.

"Not too talkative today, are you?" Deerslayer asked.

Many-Tribes groaned and rubbed his back. "Ahh, it's these old bones. They're starting to pain me. Even skunk cabbage don't help." Many-Tribes looked older; the wrinkles beneath his eyes sagged a little lower than last time. His face looked a chalky white.

Deerslayer forced out the words. "Hear about that lost kid?" Many-Tribes nodded his head as the chips flew. Deerslayer continued. "I found him! Tracked him down like an Indian, I did."

Many-Tribes interrupted, not hearing the last words. "I knew where he was all right. I could have found him easy enough."

Deerslayer looked shocked. "Why didn't you help him then? The poor kid was retarded, you know."

"I don't stick my nose in other people's business."

"He would have died out there!"

"Wouldn't be the first," Many-Tribes snapped.

Deerslayer frowned. "I don't believe you. A kid almost dies, and you carve flutes! That's great."

Many-Tribes dropped his knife and turned to Deerslayer. "They had cops in that search party. Cops and me don't mix."

"Wh—" Deerslayer caught his breath. "Why not?"

Many-Tribes leveled a steely gaze into Deerslayer's eyes. It numbed his toes. "I said we don't talk about the past here. You remember that?"

Deerslayer turned away. He kneeled beside Andy and put the deer's head in his lap. Andy's eyes sparkled; his coat of fur looked sleek. Deerslayer mumbled beneath his breath.

"Speak up, son!" the old man snapped. "You got something to say—say it!"

"I said I saw that big buck again."

"You mean the twelve-pointer?"

Deerslayer nodded, sorry that he had brought it up.

Many-Tribes tapped his temple with his finger. "I told you there ain't no such animal. It's all in your head. That deer don't live in these woods."

It did seem strange to Deerslayer. If anyone knew about deer in these woods, it was Many-Tribes. But I saw the deer, he thought. It even led me out of the woods. He did not tell Many-Tribes about that. The old man would just kid him about it—about being lost and all.

Flicking the last wood chip from his flute, Many-Tribes blew through the holes to clean them out. Then he played "Rock of Ages," which was the only tune he knew. The

87

deer looked up, puzzled. Many-Tribes banged the flute on the bench beside him. "Look, I've been rough on you today, and I'm sorry. I just haven't been feeling too well." Many-Tribes waved his arms over the area. "Someday all this will be yours." Deerslayer's mouth dropped open. Many-Tribes knelt beside him. "I'm not getting any younger, and I have no kinfolk. Someone's got to look after the deer."

Deerslayer looked up. "Don't talk foolish! You're going to live a long time. Besides, I don't know that much about deer."

"But I'm giving them to *you*. Promise me that you'll take them."

Deerslayer thought for a moment, then shook his head. "I'm not promising anything. I have my own life to sort out." He surprised himself at his directness. "Besides, didn't you tell me that deer can't be caged? No one owns them. They're as free as the winds through these pines. As free as Andy, here."

Many-Tribes let it go. "Andy will be wanting to get back to his own kind pretty soon. You understand that, don't you?"

Deerslayer did not answer. He did not want to think about it.

Many-Tribes studied him. "You have to grow up some time, Deerslayer. You have to become a man and face facts."

Deerslayer laughed and ran his fingers through his hair. "I was going to kill a deer. That's why I took the name of Deerslayer."

"What?" Many-Tribes looked puzzled.

"To become a man. I thought that by killing a deer, I would become a man."

Many-Tribe's eyes sparkled. He forgot his aches. "Any *idiot* can shoot a helpless animal. Come on, think about it. One small animal against machine guns, tanks, and bullets. It makes no sense."

"Is there a way?"

"A way for what?" Many-Tribes knew what was coming.

"To become a man. Is there any way to become a man? I mean to know it . . . really *know* it, deep inside. I heard all that garbage about facing facts and growing up. But, I mean, is there a way that *I* can know it?" Deerslayer slapped both hands against his chest.

Many-Tribes saw his cue. He lit his pipe and blew a circle of smoke into the air. "There is one way. My great-grandfather from the Apaches . . ."

Deerslayer leaped to his feet. "Tell me, Many-Tribes. It's . . . important, more important than you'll ever know."

"O.K., just settle down. To blast a deer off the face of the earth with a bullet is too easy." Many-Tribes paused, watching the anticipation build in Deerslayer's eyes. "But . . . but to touch a deer . . ."

10

ENTURIES ago, when this country rolled green, and every river sparkled drinking-clear, and flocks of passenger pigeons blocked out the sun for hours, the Indians had the same problem. How to prove a young man's courage! A boy had to prove himself to stay in the tribe. No free rides in those days. Now, some wise old man figured that anyone could shoot his enemy in the back or ride him down with a horse. That's not too brave, this old Indian figured. And of course he was right," Many-Tribes continued.

"So this Indian chief ruled that, to prove courage, a young brave had to first *touch* his enemy. Not kill or injure him—just *touch* him. Now, picture that, will ya?

"You're an Indian brave and your enemy will kill you as sure as look at you. With bow ready and tomahawk high, he waits for your head to come within striking distance. You charge. But do you shoot him from fifty yards out? Or throw rocks at him from behind your horse? No way! You run up to him, duck his weapons . . . and touch him.

That's all. Just touch him. Now, that's courage. That's how the young braves did it back then. Each touch won you a feather. Did you ever wonder why a chief always had so many feathers in his cap?

"When the Great Indian Wars ended, a different problem arose. Now what to do? Especially with no enemies around to touch." Many-Tribes relit his pipe.

Cross-legged on the ground, Deerslayer scratched his head. "I don't follow you. What does all this have to do with touching a deer?"

Many-Tribes laughed. "I'm getting there, boy, don't rush me. Now, what's the most skittish, uptight animal in these woods? Which one do you suppose is the hardest to get near?"

Deerslayer thought for a moment. "That has to be the deer."

"Right!" Many-Tribes waved his arm across the clearing. "Not these tame ones. I mean the wild ones, the really wild ones who still live by their wits. Now, if a guy could get close enough to touch one without getting mangled or what-have-you, that's courage."

Deerslayer looked up. "You mean . . . Big Buck?"

Many-Tribes nodded. "I mean any buck. If you can get close enough to *touch* him without scaring him off. Wow, that'll prove something, all right."

"I think you've hit on it. I'm going to touch that deer," Deerslayer said.

"Seeing that he don't exist, you don't stand much chance. Even if you get close enough, your hand'll probably go right through him." Many-Tribes roared with laughter, clutching his stomach.

Deerslayer flushed, jumping to his feet. "I told you that I saw him."

"You *think* you saw him, boy. Look, there's a lot of crazy things going on in these pines that man nor beast can't get a handle on. There's a lot of weirdos still living in the outback, doing a lot of crazy things. You know what I mean? Maybe your big buck is really the Jersey Devil."

"No way! Big Buck's no devil. He's flesh and blood, just like Andy here." Deerslayer draped an arm over the yearling.

"Right!" Many-Tribes sneered. "If you say so . . ."

"Forget it then! Let's just forget I ever brought it up. If what you say is true—about touching a deer—how do I go about it? How do I get close enough?"

"That, my stubborn young friend, is up to you to find out. A word of advice though. First, study their ways until you think like them. Know their every move, what they eat, where they sleep. Learn to hold your breath for ten minutes. Practice walking without touching the ground, until you can do it as softly as the junco and as silently as a wisp of smoke."

Deerslayer hoisted Andy over his shoulders and turned to leave. "That's exactly what I'm going to do, Many-Tribes. I'm going to touch that deer, if it's the last thing I do."

"Good luck!" Many-Tribes waved. The flute sounds of "Rock of Ages" followed Deerslayer from the clearing. Once he was past the thicket wall, the sound stopped as if it only existed in another world. Deerslayer felt healthy and strong. The talk had given him a purpose—something to sink his teeth into. Andy felt lighter on his shoulders. Deerslayer was not even breathing hard when he entered his campsite.

Deerslayer started with the fox sparrows. Squatting in the meadow, he watched their every move until they made sense. Boy, were they nervous, always looking around! I can't understand why they don't have ulcers, he thought. They never stopped moving. Deerslayer sat with his open palms flat against the ground. He placed seeds in each hand and waited. Hour after hour. One sparrow came close, but never too close. Deerslayer studied its many colors. It had a rust-colored tail, and brown spots on its white breast. Except for the brown spots, it looked like a run-of-the-mill sparrow. It scratched in the ground, always moving, always searching.

Somehow the word got out. After the third day, twenty sparrows scampered around Deerslayer, still keeping a safe distance. They took a few seeds that he had thrown in a wide circle around him. He stayed still until his muscles throbbed. He forced himself to calm down, to become part of his surroundings, like a blade of grass or a waving dandelion. He knew that he had to become one with nature before the sparrows would trust him.

On the fourth morning, he grew impatient. This is a waste of time, he thought. Sitting around to watch the grass grow. It's stupid! He had never sat this still this long in school. Why now? Maybe touching a deer was not such a good idea after all. Just when he was about to give up, a bird hopped closer. Deerslayer froze and waited it out.

Three sparrows, probably babies, hopped within three feet of his open hands. An older, wiser bird squawked behind them, but they did not listen. The fledglings, like

Deerslayer, had to find out for themselves. A dragonfly, with its long blue tail bent like a bow, settled on Deerslayer's nose. It tickled, but he did not move. Squinting cross-eyed, he watched the dragonfly grab a foothold. He wanted to sneeze and laugh at the same time. But not after three days, he thought. The large eyes, like carpet tacks, stared back at him. In one quick move, Deerslayer blinked his eyes without moving his head. The dragonfly caught the message and buzzed off. The birds hopped closer.

Like a dog sniffing a tree, one bird pecked at Deerslayer's finger. He did not move. The bird hopped on his hand and pecked at the seeds. Sensing no danger, it gobbled a mouthful in its bill. Seeing that one brave warrior had broken the ice, other sparrows landed on Deerslayer. Excited, Deerslayer slowly released his breath through the corner of his mouth with a slow hiss. Before long, thirty fox sparrows hopped over him as though he were a bird feeder.

"Yahoo!" he yelled, leaping up. The birds whirlpooled away, glad to escape with their lives. "I did it!" Deerslayer yelled.

The older wiser bird squawked from its tree, as if to say I told you so.

Squirrels came next. He sat in the low-hanging branches of their favorite gathering place and froze, becoming part of the tree itself. The squirrels had a field day. Deerslayer had them eating out of his hand in four hours. Rabbits proved tougher.

Deerslayer lay down on their runs, but they gave him a wide detour. Half dozing on the ground one day, he felt a wet nose sniffing his ear. He came to his senses quietly, just opening one eye at a time, a trick he had learned with the sparrows. The nose belonged to a rabbit, as cute and plump as any he saw. That night, he fed Andy double rations. The yearling's limp had all but gone. But Andy had a sad look in his eyes. Deerslayer rubbed him behind the ears, thinking about something else. Tomorrow was the big day!

Deerslayer chose a deer run that crossed the pines, wove its way through a stand of cedar, then ended by the marsh. He knew the deer drank before and after their feed, both at sunup and sunset. He picked a spot where the run narrowed to pass between large bushes. He crouched within the leaves of the largest bush and waited. And waited.

The deer did not pass that evening. The next day he waited at the same spot. A buck, two does, and a fawn usually drank at the marsh. Deerslayer shook his head. Where were they? Up the run, he heard a crash. Something headed his way. He crouched on his heels, ready to spring forward to touch the deer. Perspiration poured into his eyes. He blinked it away. The noise sounded like a stampede. Whatever was coming his way either was too large for the run or crashed off the trail. Bushes and trees shook as in a windstorm. The hooves pounded closer. Deerslayer felt a strong wind brush past his face, but saw nothing. The crashing flew by him, grew fainter, then disappeared around a far bend.

An hour later he saw a buck—the small one with velvet still clinging to its new growth of antlers. Ever watchful, it led a group along the trail. Steady! Deerslayer wheezed. Steady! He could hardly believe it as the group trotted closer. Less than two weeks, and already he would prove his manhood. Old Many-Tribes will flip out, he thought. About five strides away, the buck suddenly spun in its tracks. The others followed, showing white tails, until all that was left of them was a dust cloud. Deerslayer rubbed his eyes in disbelief. Something had spooked them, he thought. But what?

As one day blended into the next like the ripples of a stream, Andy grew more and more restless. He stood at the base of the hill, looking past the field into the distant stand of pitch pine. He stopped eating. Deerslayer began to worry. He ran his hands over Andy's back. The skin quivered and shook like the hide of a cow shooing flies. Andy's white tail stood up, something Deerslayer had never seen before, and he walked away. Halfway across the meadow, Andy twisted his head over his shoulder for a last look, then he sank into the darkening underbrush.

Three days passed and still no Andy. This was the longest he had ever stayed away. Deerslayer grew more concerned. He even forgot about touching the deer for now. Andy's going left an empty spot in his life. Maybe he has joined his friends at the deer farm, he thought.

Deerslayer headed for Many-Tribes. He knew the trail by heart, even in the bending shadows. He stopped short at the entrance. Something was wrong. The branches that covered the hidden entrance to the clearing were broken, the bushes torn back. An empty beer can lay off to one side. Deerslayer leaned forward on the path, listening. Up ahead, a motorcycle crashed through the bushes, kicking up a trail of dirt . . . whining and spitting sparks. It headed straight for him.

11

T HE boy rolled over the ground to avoid the screaming motorcycle. Its rider hunched low over the handlebars. The wheels kicked dirt into Deerslayer's face and mouth. He choked. Down the road, the Suzuki 185 turned and headed back to the clearing. The rider never saw him. From beneath the bushes, off the trail, Deerslayer saw the heavy jackboots and chains of the rider.

Keeping off the trail, Deerslayer crawled to the field. Two motorcycles circled the cabin, churning up grass sod and clumps of dirt. The field was a shambles. The riders spun their wheels toward the cabin, then turned sharply, sending up a wide spray of dirt over the shack.

"Let's get some more beer!" one yelled. He sat low in his seat, almost lying down. Both popped wheelies and disappeared down the run until the sound of their backfires was lost in the night.

All was still. At the far end of the field, a lone cricket cried out. Then another. Soon the entire meadow, which now looked like a battlefield, sang out with insects.

Behind Deerslayer, the bullfrogs joined the chorus. Then the low hoot of an owl. Deerslayer raced for the cabin.

Inside, some wood chips smoldered from a toppled candle. The hungry flames chewed into the wood. Grabbing a deerskin, Deerslayer whacked out the fire. Many-Tribes moaned in a corner, holding his forehead in both hands. Deerslayer pried away his fingers and saw an ugly red gash on the right side of his head.

"Let's go, Many-Tribes!" he snapped.

Many-Tribes looked around, dazed. "Go? Where?"

"To town! We have to get you to a doctor," Deerslayer said.

Many-Tribes shook away the cobwebs in his brain, then shoved Deerslayer's hand aside. "Town? No way!"

"But you're hurt badly. Skunk cabbage won't help this one," Deerslayer said.

Rising slowly, Many-Tribes relit his candle and placed it on the table. "Can't do that, Deerslayer. I made my choice a long time ago. I chose to leave town behind me. I'm not about to change because of a little head wound."

Tears welled in Deerslayer's eyes. "But it looks bad. We have to get help."

Many-Tribes did not answer. He shook his head. "Ohhh! Hand me that bucket of water in the corner." He soaked a strip of hide in the water and tied it around his head. "Ohhh, I feel like I was scalped. What happened?"

Deerslayer told him about the two bike riders. Many-Tribes wrinkled his brow. "Used to be an empty land, no one around for miles. But now, with those dumb bikes, nuts like that can tear up my cabin and be home for supper." Slowly he shook his head. "Times sure have changed."

Deerslayer held his tongue, then could wait no longer. "Well, what are we going to do about it?"

Many-Tribes laughed. "Do about it? What *can* we do about it? Go to the police?" Many-Tribes roared on the floor. "What did you do after the dogs attacked you? Did you go after them?"

"No! They were too much for me."

"And what does a rabbit do after escaping the hawk? Does he sprout wings to hunt down his enemy?" Many-Tribes grunted. "To answer your question, I'm not going to do anything about it."

"Come on, Many-Tribes. You have to do something. You just can't let those creeps come in and mess up your place."

"Why not?"

Deerslayer thought for a moment. "I don't know exactly. But it's just not manly to sit back and forget about it."

Many-Tribes frowned. "I told you what it takes to be a man. Will you track down your enemies the rest of your life only to pop them in the head? Or wreck their homes? Boy, you'd be as stupid as they are. Don't you see that? The only way out is to touch the deer. How many times must I tell you that? Ohhh!" Many-Tribes rubbed his temples, which now began to swell. A slight trickle of blood dripped over his shoulder.

Deerslayer knitted his brow. "They will return, you know."

"Maybe so! Maybe not! But I'm not going to lose any sleep over maybes."

Deerslayer stood up. "Well, I'm going to take action. I just can't sit around and do nothing."

99

Many-Tribes grabbed him by the shoulders. "No! Don't you see that you're falling into the trap? You'll be as dumb as they and continue the whole thing."

Deerslayer shrugged his shoulders, and headed for the door. "I gotta do something, Many-Tribes."

"Touch the deer then. Prove you're a man."

"That's dumb and you know it." Deerslayer bolted from the cabin. Many-Tribes yelled after him. He ran into the thicket and picked up the trail. The bikes had plowed through the undergrowth like a dinosaur in pain. The trail was so wide, it was like following the turnpike. About daybreak, Deerslayer heard voices in the distance.

"Let's go back and bug the old man!" Both riders ate beans from a can with their fingers. Their bikes rested on their sides. Deerslayer crept around until he was between them and the swamp, which stood about five-hundred yards away.

Deerslayer stood up in the trail and yelled. "Hey, you slobs! I can smell you from here to China."

"Wha—" Both leaped for their bikes and gunned for Deerslayer. By now he was halfway down the trail. The twists and turns and fallen logs slowed down the bikes, as Deerslayer had figured.

"Wait'll we get you, kid! We're gonna put you out in the sun to dry. Gonna pick you clean like a catfish." The bikes churned dirt in all directions.

The trail ran wide for a distance, then narrowed beneath some overhanging grapevines. Once past the underbrush, Deerslayer cut a sharp left. Straight ahead lay the swamp and . . . mud.

The riders did not know what hit them. They crashed

through the undergrowth, carrying lengths of twisting vines behind them, and sailed ten feet into the air.

"NOOO!" The bikes landed in the swamp with a loud splat and slowly sank to the hubcaps. "OHHH, NOO!"

Deerslayer held both hands over his mouth. Mud dripped over everything, their bikes, their helmets, their clothes. "Ohhh, nooo!" one kept screaming.

It took two hours to wheel their slimy machines onto dry land. Everything dripped mud and smelled just as bad. "Ohh, noo!"

The large rider exploded. "Stop saying that, dodo. Let's get these bikes into shape." Without pausing, he stripped down the carburetor to clean it out.

"Oh, no!"

"I said—" The big rider cut his sentence short. "Did you hear that?"

The other rider smeared some mud from his mouth. "Hear what?"

"Listen!"

"I don't hear anything!"

"If you'd shut up for a minute, you might, dimwit!" He tilted his head toward the forest. "There! Did you hear that?"

Dimwit shook his head. The low growls exploded into roars all around them. From behind the trees and beneath the laurel bushes. The mean, hungry growls of wild dogs!

From his lookout, Deerslayer knew they were there before he heard their growls. The signs were everywhere. Crickets had stopped chirping; frogs had dived underwater. He crept toward the pack. By now both riders hugged each other from behind their bikes.

"Help me!" Dimwit cried.

"If you'd let go of me, I might help you," the big rider snapped. But the other one did not let go. He could not let go.

About ten paces from the bikes, Deerslayer broke through the bushes, then stopped short. The lean police dog sat on his haunches in the middle of the trail, leering at Deerslayer. Waiting.

"You knew," Deerslayer whispered. "You knew I was here all the time."

A trickle of foam oozed down the corner of the dog's mouth. His growl cut short the yelps of the other dogs. They turned from the shaking riders to watch.

The two circled each other like boxers. Deerslayer crouched low with bent knees, arms forward. He kept moving his open hands to distract the police dog. The dog faked a leap, then pulled back, still circling. Each boxer searched for a weakness in the other's defense, ready to pounce at the first opening.

"Haww!" Deerslayer lunged forward, then withdrew. The dog did not take the feint, but instead held his ground. A turkey buzzard soared overhead, landing on the uppermost branch of a dead cedar. A mother rabbit shooed her babies into their den. A praying mantis blended into the stalk of a marsh reed.

Deerslayer bounced on the balls of his feet. One foot sank into the underground tunnel of a mole. He pitched backward.

The lead dog saw the opening. Taking a running start, he sprang into the air with bared teeth.

Half stumbling, Deerslayer shot a knee into the dog's

chest, and brought his elbow down. It struck the dog on the side of the head. The dog landed in a heap on the ground, rolled over once, but quickly regained his feet.

Deerslayer tried to take advantage. He kicked his leg sideways against the dog's head. The dog brushed it aside with his paw—jabbing, jabbing. Opening his mouth, he clamped his fangs onto Deerslayer's sneaker.

Quickly Deerslayer fell to the ground and twisted his foot and the dog's head in one motion. The dog released his grip with a whine.

The entire Pine Barrens fell silent as the air froze and the creeks stopped running. Except for the swamp. Except for the bikers. Except for Deerslayer and the police dog.

Two sets of eyes gave no signs of weakness. Two sets of eyes blazed red in a fight for survival. Only one would walk away from this fight, and they both knew it.

Then Deerslayer blinked for only a second. But it was enough. The police dog leaped, this time snapping his teeth inches away from Deerslayer's cheek. As the dog sailed past, Deerslayer clasped both fists together, and came down with all his might. The dull crunch of a broken neck frightened the turkey buzzard. It took flight over the swamp into the clouds.

The other dogs looked at each other, puzzled. The cocker spaniel moaned, its tail between its legs. They circled for a minute, sniffed their fallen leader, who did not growl. He did not snap at them, and the dogs felt happy. One by one they drifted into the blackening shadows, away from the fight.

Deerslayer had three claw marks down the center of his

chest. Thin streams of blood flowed freely. He rubbed them and smiled. Only surface cuts. A little sphagnum moss will take care of them.

Awkwardly the riders untangled themselves, one from the other, and approached Deerslayer.

"Hey, man! I . . ." Without another word, the big one picked up his bike and walked it around the marsh toward town.. Dimwit followed.

Deerslayer sucked in a mouthful of cedar air and splashed swamp water over his body. He was still shaking. He looked at the dog, lying there on the ground. Thin, hungry . . . half dead before the fight. Deerslayer felt it his duty to bury the fallen warrior. He dug a three-foot hole with his hands and buried the dog in the soft sand. He cried silently to himself. The owl did not hear his sobs.

The next morning he returned to Many-Tribes, who walked in the clearing with an empty look in his eyes. Like the look of the deer—deep and black, but empty. Deerslayer helped himself to the mixture of skunk cabbage and moss. The wounds might scar, he thought. But it's too late to worry about that now. He told Many-Tribes about the fight and about the riders in the mud. Many-Tribes did not seem to hear. He kept muttering something to himself.

Deerslayer forced him to sit down and then fed him. He had to shove the food into Many-Tribes' mouth. Some food took; some dribbled down the front of the old man's shirt.

"No sense anymore," he mumbled. Deerslayer leaned closer to hear. "Have to go sometime, have to give up.

Can't fight any more." Many-Tribes leaped to his feet, and shook a clenched fist at the sky. "Can't fight any more!"

Deerslayer eased him back into the seat and draped an arm around the bony shoulders. "What can I do, Many-Tribes? Tell me what to do." Deerslayer looked into his eyes. For a second Deerslayer saw that old sparkle, the devil grin that he had seen the first day they met.

"Touch the deer, boy! That'll make things right."

Deerslayer held his head between his hands. Should I take him back to town, he asked himself. Should I leave him here like he wants? Deerslayer moaned. Russ would know what to do, he thought. Russ was a weirdo with a potbelly and all, but he was good in emergencies. He'd know what to do, Deerslayer thought. He wondered what Russ was doing at that moment.

12

YOU can't call off the search now, sheriff. Not when we're so close." Russ Kochak paced the floor inside police headquarters, off Route 9. The office had once been a beauty parlor; it stood in the heart of Munsey near the main roads.

The sheriff pulled at his lower lip. "Russ . . . Russ. It's been weeks, and still no trace of your boy. What do you want from me?" He talked past Russ, his eyes on the wall clock. It was already ten minutes after lunchtime.

"My boy is out there . . . somewhere. We've got to find him."

The sheriff looked grim. "We've looked. We had the National Guard out there." He counted off on his fingers: "We had helicopters patrol the area. We had volunteer firemen, the boy scouts, the chamber of commerce. These guys all have jobs and families, you know. You can't expect them to keep up this search for a month."

"Why not? You keep looking until we find him. Is that too much to ask?" Russ snapped.

"Yes, it is too much to ask. Look . . ." The sheriff led Russ to a swivel chair. "Sit down and listen. You know as well as I that there are parts of the Pine Barrens that no one has ever seen. Face facts—we'll never find him. Just last month some hunters found a skeleton in one of the shacks back there. Well, we never did find that shack again. And those hunters were experienced woodsmen."

Russ melted into the chair. "I have to keep looking, sheriff. I have to find . . . my son. I failed once, but I'm not going to fail again."

The sheriff looked puzzled. "What are you talking about?"

"You knew Sarah, my first wife, didn't you?"

The sheriff nodded. "Tragic, the way she walked out on you and Aimee."

"Well, it was my failure too. I had something to do with her walking out. I can't let that happen again. I can't watch another family die."

"But you hardly knew the boy, Russ."

"He's my *son* whether for a day, or a year. He has no one out there, sheriff. He's alone and scared. I have to keep looking."

The sheriff checked the wall clock again. "Look, I can't start the search again unless you give me some hard proof that Robert is still alive . . . I'm sorry."

"Talking to you is like talking to the wall." Russ leaped from the chair, picked up the telephone, and dialed.

"Who are you calling?" the sheriff asked.

"Don't worry—it's a local call." Russ threw a quarter on the desk. "Here, I'll pay for it." The phone rang twice. Someone picked it up at the other end.

107

Russ spoke. "The Commander, please . . . Hello, Commander Grimach. Look, this is the sheriff's office. I want you to continue that search for the missing boy. Right, the Kochak boy! Send your helicopters—"

The sheriff grabbed the phone and slammed down the receiver.

"You're going to end in jail if you keep this up. Now stop it!"

Russ fell back into the chair. "I have to do something."

The sheriff opened the top drawer of his desk and thumbed through an address book. "I doubt if this'll help, but here's the address of that boy we recently found in the woods. Scott—something." He wrote down the address on a slip of paper. "We couldn't get anything out of him. But why don't you give it a try?"

Clutching the address in a shaky hand, Russ knocked on the front door. The screen was broken, and toys cluttered the front lawn. A woman with a drawn face peeked through a curtain in the window.

"I'm Russ Kochak, father of that missing boy. I wonder if I could speak to Scott for a few minutes."

"Sure!" The pale woman in the faded wraparound led Russ into the living room. Scott sat on the floor in front of the television set with his Superman doll. The room was dark. He did not look up as Russ knelt beside him.

"Scott, my boy is lost in the woods like you were. Did you see a boy anywhere out there?"

The woman crossed her arms in front of her and looked at the ceiling. "He won't talk, you know. He doesn't even understand you."

Russ ignored her. "Scott, you have to help me. If you saw anything . . . *anything*, you have to tell me." He looked into the boy's large eyes, but saw nothing. No hint of understanding. No movement. Nothing. "Scott . . . think. Think hard."

The woman wiped her hands on her apron. "I think you better go now, Mr. Kochak. If you get him upset, I have to clean up the mess. I have to take care of him. No one helps *me*."

"But Scott is the only one who can help. He was there. Maybe he saw something," Russ said.

"If he did, he can't say. You're lucky to have a normal boy. You're lucky that you don't have to wake up each morning and see your son waste away before your eyes."

"My son is lost. I have to find him."

The woman rubbed her eyes. "There is one thing. The sheriff said that Scott cried out for help in those woods."

"So?" Russ looked puzzled.

"So, there's no way that Scott could cry for help. He hasn't made a sound in ten years."

On his way back to police headquarters, Russ picked up Aimee, who was eating lunch at a friend's house. She wore a faded sunsuit—slightly soiled. It had not been easy for him, coping alone.

"Let's go."

"Are we going to the hospital again?" she asked.

"No, this is more important," he said, leading her into the police station. The sheriff slapped his open hand against his head at the sight of Russ.

The words tumbled out; the sheriff only caught a few of

them: "New information . . . Scott did not cry for help . . . someone else did . . . it could be Robert."

Sadly the sheriff shook his head from side to side. "We've been through all this already. Robert is lost, and that's that."

"But you said that you'll open up the search with new information," Russ snapped. "Well, I gave you some."

"Not good enough, Russ. Again, I'm sorry. There is nothing I can do."

"Well, there's something I can do," Russ said, over his shoulder. "Come on, Aimee."

She looked up and frowned. "Not Pine Lake again! We've been there every day since the accident."

"And we'll keep going there every day until we find Robert. He loved Pine Lake. If he returns, that's the place he'll be." Russ stormed from the office, nearly bumping into two motorcycle riders. They were ragged and dirty, and they had a strange story to tell the sheriff.

13

BENEATH the rhododendron bush beside the deer run, Deerslayer nibbled some berries. His stomach growled from hunger. He had been up since long before sunrise, waiting for the deer. Through half-opened eyes, he watched the morning sun stretch its long fingers across the woods. He first heard the birds singing overhead, then the scurrying of squirrels on the leafy floor. A chipmunk shot past him not a foot away, unafraid.

Down the run by the twisted oak trotted the buck. He moved straight ahead, looking from side to side, ever alert. The two does followed close behind. Deerslayer rested on one elbow. Before he could move into position, the three deer had already passed him. A speckled fawn lagged behind with dainty steps.

The fawn bent its head close to the ground and nibbled the acorns that Deerslayer had scattered on the trail. Jawing away, it did not notice the slight movement in the bushes. Up ahead, one of the does nervously pawed the ground. The fawn paid no attention.

111

With a mighty leap, Deerslayer sprang through the bushes with both hands out. They struck the fawn's back and slid down its flank before hitting the ground. The startled creature tore after its mother, not recognizing the strange form that was rolling on the ground behind.

"I did it! I touched the deer!" the strange form screamed to the skies. Deerslayer jumped up and down with joy, then pulled at his nose. "Practice is over. Now for the big one," he said. "Big Buck!"

Deerslayer hiked back to the spot near the marsh where he had last seen the giant deer. Big Buck did not use a regular run like the other deer. He was too smart—always changing his trails, always moving in different directions. Deerslayer prepared himself for a long battle.

Over a trail, near its narrowest point, there grew a pitch pine. The stunted tree sent its twisting branches across the trail. Deerslayer climbed up and pressed flat against the largest branch. Thick clusters of pine needles hid him from view. He dangled one arm down through the branches over the run and waited. The sun climbed two hands in the east.

Deerslayer drifted off, there in the tree. He felt healthy and strong. He admired his arm, now tanned to a deep bronze like the color of a dead oak leaf. He remembered back, back when his arm once was as white and lifeless as snow. Back with his family. Back before the accident. The events flooded his mind, there in the tree. He did not fight them this time. He let them flow.

He saw the crash and heard the shattered metal. He saw his mother's face on the roadside. He saw himself kneeling beside her, saying, "It's all right, Mom. It's all right now." Instead of being frightened and angry and choked up as before, he remained calm, there in the tree. What happened, happened, he thought. Nothing can change that. He knew that now.

Down the trail, what seemed like a small tornado twisted leaves and twigs into the air. A high-pitched whine changed into a roar, coming closer. Waking from his trance, Deerslayer braced himself. Through the haze of pine needles, he first saw the massive antlers, shining in the sun. Big Buck moved closer, moving half the forest in his wake.

Hold your breath for ten minutes. Walk without touching the ground. Deerslayer remembered the advice of Many-Tribes. He tried, as he dangled his arm above the run. Through an opening in the branches he saw the giant deer. It stood much larger than he had imagined. Muscle rippled over muscle beneath the heavy skin. The eyes were two black dots of pure energy, the nose a glistening mass of steam. Leaves swirled around the deer like pilot fish around a shark; clouds of dust hid the pounding hooves.

An antler slapped against Deerslayer's outstretched hand, then the deep fur of the deer's back. Big Buck stopped there beneath the tree. Deerslayer's fingers froze over the sleek fur. A bolt of warmth shot up his arm like an electric current. In that brief second Deerslayer thought, "Why not?"

Letting go of the branch, he rolled onto the deer's back. He wrapped his arms and legs around the huge body. He buried his face in the deer's neck.

Big Buck bolted like a blast of lightning and flew down the trail. Leaping over a tree jam, the deer crashed off the trail into deeper woods. Branches slapped across his back, but Deerslayer held on. He felt the deer's hot breath pass over him; he heard the heavy snorting in the rush. He felt every nerve and muscle explode beneath him, but he held on.

Big Buck raced past the marsh reeds and the bullfrogs. He raced past the moonshiner's still and the old shack. He raced past cedar stands and clover fields. He raced past a rabbit den and beneath an osprey's nest. And Deerslayer held on.

Big Buck charged into a dense undergrowth of thorn bushes that ripped Deerslayer's face and hands. A length of vine snagged on the antlers and trailed behind like a banner. Still Big Buck raced on. He raced past the cranberry bog, and the foundations of a dead town. Past an old railroad siding and the ruins of a chimney. Past a covey of quail and a colonial graveyard. And Deerslayer held on.

Deerslayer's breath came hot and fast. He felt so alive, so charged with new energy. Things would never be quite the same after this. Nothing would remain as before. In the mad rush, Deerslayer saw a hundred Indian braves touch a hundred deer and dance around a hundred campfires with their newly won feathers. And he saw himself holding the largest feather of them all—an eagle's tail feather. Big Buck carried him over hill and river, through day and night, and through the present and past. And Deerslayer held on.

As he pictured the Indian chief placing the eagle

feather in his hand, he felt his grip weakening. He dug his fingers like claws into the deer's flank. The fur was dripping with perspiration, slippery to the touch. Deerslayer kept slipping.

"Hang on!" he yelled out loud. He felt his body sliding over the deer's back.

Now Big Buck crashed through a thick stand of cedars, its antlers knifing a path. Deerslayer's fingers turned numb; he lost all feeling in his arms. His thighs felt locked into position. He slipped over the deer's rump. Big Buck bucked through the woods, still charging straight ahead. The deer ducked beneath a low-hanging branch. It brushed Deerslayer off the deer's back onto the ground. He rolled over in the sand before blacking out.

Half dazed, he awoke with both arms and legs wrapped around a moss-covered log, and his face buried in damp oak leaves. Sitting up, he shook his head. Then he remembered.

"I DID IT!" he screamed. "I TOUCHED THE DEER!" Almost out of his mind, he raced for the camp of Many-Tribes, which was nearby. He could not believe it. "I not only touched a deer. I touched Big Buck, the biggest, meanest, most kingly deer this side of Munsey."

"I did it! I did it!" he yelled, running into the camp. A wave of nervousness rolled through the deer, but upon seeing Deerslayer, they returned to their feeding. Deerslayer touched each deer as he dashed to the cabin. The touch was not the same. No feeling was the same as when he had touched Big Buck.

Many-Tribes lay on his bunk inside the cabin. Once through the doorway, Deerslayer exploded—the words tumbled out like a waterfall. "Sure I was a little scared, but I waited until he was right below me. Then I pounced. Wow, what a moment! I jumped right on his back. He took off like a rocket, but I held on. It wasn't easy, Many-Tribes, but I held on."

Many-Tribes offered no grunts, no signs of approval. He lay on the bunk as Deerslayer continued. "You were right—all the time, you were right. You've got to *face* your problem and hang on. That deer crashed through everything to throw me. I hugged him so tightly I thought his heart was my heart, his breath my breath. He tried every trick in the book, but I held on."

Deerslayer repeated his story three times before coming up for air. His excitement flashed from his eyes. He shot a glance at the old man. "Well, aren't you going to say anything? I mean, I actually *touched* the deer. That makes me a brave, doesn't it? Ha!" he laughed. "Break out the feathers, Many-Tribes. I made it, just like you said."

Many-Tribes lay on the bunk.

Deerslayer ran to his side, kneeling beside the bunk. "Many-Tribes," he whispered. "I made it. I touched the deer." Many-Tribes lay on the bunk.

"MANY-TRIBES!" Deerslayer yelled. He shook the old man by the shoulders. "MANY-TRIBES!" No reply. He fell across the old man's chest, which did not rise and fall with each breath. "No . . . No! Don't go. Not *now*!" Many-Tribes lay on the bunk.

Deerslayer wanted to cry, but the tears hung in his eyes. His body went limp. He placed his lips close to Many-Tribes' ear and whispered, "You said it'd be O.K.

116

You said if I touched the deer, that it'll be O.K. You said
. . ." Deerslayer could hold back no longer. He cried; his
sobs shook the old man's chest.

Finally he rose, staring down at his friend.

"Robert!" he suddenly blurted. "My name is Robert!"

He smeared the old man's body with the mixture of
skunk cabbage and sphagnum moss, its magic gone. He
wrapped him in his beloved deerskins and placed a
feather in his wrinkled hand. He laid the flute beside him
on the bunk.

A gray-winged goshawk with red eyes looked down
over the clearing from the top branch of the tallest cedar.
Its eyes followed a wood duck below, flying to a nearby
pond for safety. The goshawk leaped straight up into the
air, then dove down, down at fifty miles an hour toward
the unsuspecting duck. A split second before impact, the
goshawk twisted its body and sank its talons home. As
simple as that! One second flying home, and the next . . .
Quick, clean, and over. The wood duck did not get a
chance to cry.

Robert did not notice the goshawk, which was rare in
those parts, but he knew about the fight. It happened
every day in the Barrens. Even people did not escape the
struggle to survive.

It took only a few minutes to splash the deer fat over the
cabin, both inside and out. Robert stepped back and lit
the match. The fire caught, slowly at first. The deer hides,
the walls, then the roof. Before long, the entire cabin
ignited into black smoke, which swiftly rose into the
overhead clouds.

Robert shed no tears, said no prayers. He just watched

the black smoke and the white clouds and the blue sky. A few sparks fell on the marsh grass, but its dampness quickly put them out. The cabin became a holocaust as Robert watched, kneeling on the ground a safe distance away. The flames danced in his eyes. The fire burned red, and the dry cedar logs crashed into red ashes.

Satisfied, the goshawk returned to its tree to watch the smoke. The few remaining deer watched with wide-open eyes, then turned to leave. There were other clearings and other fields.

14

ROBERT emptied the stored baskets of dried berries onto the field at the base of the hill. "Maybe now the deer will return." He had not seen any since the burning of the cabin. It was as though the deer went with Many-Tribes into the clouds.

On the first day back at his camp, Robert collected all his traps. He broke them into small pieces and buried the pieces beneath the twisted roots of an oak tree. Even the frog nets. He lived on greens . . . roots, leaves, stalks—whatever. Not the best diet in the world, but he survived.

He spent long, dreamy afternoons in the meadow in the freeze position. The birds flew in and around his open arms. Even the barn swallows paused in their zigzag flights to rest on his shoulders. A redwing blackbird waddled beside him; a mother robin pulled worms at his feet. He did not move.

Five squirrels, one with only half a tail, played tag beneath his legs. A mother rabbit wrinkled her nose at him, then nibbled a dandelion blossom. Robert gaped at the animals' sleek beauty. They had nothing but themselves and one another, yet they walked with heads held high. Proud to be alive. Proud to be part of the whole. Robert knew each creature by name, and, for a fleeting second, he felt part of the Great Family. He belonged. But the feeling quickly vanished. These creatures were wild, and he was not. He realized that now.

One night after a heavy rainstorm, the roof caved in. Instead of repairing it, he just moved his clump of bedding to a dry spot. Often at night he smelled the grass scent of Andy beside him. He missed Andy.

Something had changed, and the world looked different. Something inside his head made him feel awkward here in the woods. He could not explain it. Whatever it was, it had happened after Andy left. Or was it when he had fought the dog? Or when Many-Tribes died? No, he thought, it happened when he had touched the deer. But he could not be sure.

Wildlife exploded all around him. The animals survived with or without him. It did not make him sad. He was just one small grain of sand in the scheme of things. One day, from afar, he spied Andy staring at him through the leaves of a pepper bush.

"Andy!" he yelled, but the yearling held fast. It just stared. Something behind those liquid eyes hinted a feeling . . . a longing, but it trotted away.

Robert shoved his books and equipment into the deer hide cape, muttering to himself. He felt so strange. So weird! Maybe it was better that Andy did not recognize him. He wondered if Andy felt as depressed as he did.

Robert's sadness grew deeper, until he barely ate. One morning, he left his campsite and headed east into the sun.

The burned section of woods had come alive again. New scrub oak shoots grew from parent roots. Spikes of pitch pine peppered the ground. Pixie moss and Virginia creepers covered everything. Sheep laurel plants with their curly leaves pushed upward through the ashes. Animals scurried across the trail in front of him. Although once dead, the forest was returning anew in all its splendor.

The loud croaking of the frogs erupted in the marsh, whose waters had risen from the recent thunderstorm. The current from the feed creek moved faster. White water lilies fringed the still, stagnant pond. He laughed at the thought of the bike riders in the mud bath. Their jackboots were probably still stuck in the bottom mud.

Robert bit his lip as he skidded a stick across the mud flat. The frogs still croaked; the dragonflies still skated across the stagnant surface. Why not? he thought. They did not know Many-Tribes.

Farther down the trail, Robert passed the makeshift grave of the police dog. He felt no anger for him, only pity. He pulled some weeds around the area before moving on. That night he slept on a bed of pine needles.

The next day Robert passed the foundation of his first home in the woods—the hunters' shack. A sweet pepper bush turned yellow; the leaves of an uprooted oak turned a deep brown. Red clusters of new maple shoots clawed through the burned timbers. Mushrooms clung to the

121

logs and overturned roots. The Pine Barrens grew over the crumbling cinder blocks, which now looked so small, so fragile, so out of place. In a few years, the shack would be a mound of earth and a memory.

Still farther on, Robert stopped by the skeleton shack, as he called it. The small clearing was completely trampled, as if a herd of horses had gone berserk. Large planks were nailed across each window and the door. A large police sign stood to one side of the front path. KEEP OUT! POLICE AREA!

"They must have found the bones," he said aloud. He cringed at the thought of that grinning skull and the spider's web in the rib cage. Even in death, there is life, he thought.

For three days he walked in a trance. He followed the same trail which first had led him into the woods. He could not shake the longing inside. Each time he tried to pin it down, it drifted into smoke. Each time he tried to put it into words, it left him and he could not pull it back. Some deep yearning pulled him back to the spot where it had first started. *His mother died.* So did Many-Tribes. He accepted it now. That was that!

Hanging heavy between the heady aroma of decaying oak leaves and pine needles was the sharp smell of burning chicken. His nostrils quivered.

"Haven't smelled that in a long time," he muttered. "When was the last time?" He parted some low-hanging branches and walked through, the branches snapping against his back. "The Moose barbecue!" It flooded back in an instant, as if a floodgate had just opened in his mind. The Father and Son Big Eat with Russ!

His eyes teared. Russ tried, he thought, but I didn't help him at all. It was not easy for him either. The idea surprised Robert. A new wife! A new kid . . . and a stubborn one at that! Robert bit his lip and stamped on a dry stick that broke with a crack. A blue jay, disturbed in his meal, protested in a nearby tree. Robert gritted his teeth and pressed onward.

The mouth-watering smell of barbecued chicken grew stronger as Robert parted the thicket on the far side of Pine Lake. Bordered on three sides by trees and bushes, the lake sparkled in the afternoon sun. At the north end, two weeping willows dipped their dainty branches, like drinking deer, into the clear water. At its narrowest point, the lake measured forty yards across. On the far side, in the brush, Robert watched the picnickers and the bathers.

Some swimmers ran along the edge of the white sand. A small boy carried a dead fish to his mother. A woman sunbathed by an overturned rowboat. Two teenagers tossed a football by the parking lot on the hill. Some people splashed in the shallow waters, while a few swam to the raft. A young girl dived from the raft in Robert's direction. His eyes scanned past her and stopped at the parking lot across the lake.

Cars! The accident flooded back, but only for a moment. He had to fight it!

The girl, about Aimee's age, paddled in the deep end of the lake, past the raft nearest to Robert. Robert drifted off again, watching the girl, but not hearing the splashing water. For a moment the lake turned silent.

Aimee! he thought. What must she be going through?

A new mother! A wise-guy new brother who runs away at the first sign of trouble.

The girl, her twisted hair matting her face, swam closer to the near shore. Robert, from his hidden position, watched silently.

Real people, he thought. These were his own kind. The rabbits had other rabbits; the deer had other deer. He had Aimee and Russ.

The snapping of a twig behind him caused his head to spin around. There, beyond the thicket, with steaming nostrils and burning eyes, stood Big Buck. Its large empty eyes looked through Robert. The deer looked ready to run again, to play another game.

Robert smiled. "I don't need you anymore, fella." Big Buck seemed to understand. He sank into the surrounding woods.

Robert knew that he would always be there, if he ever needed him. Behind every tree in the Pine Barrens. Behind each bush and waving clump of marsh grass. Every time a breeze shook a scrub pine, it would be Big Buck. Every time a twig snapped in the forest at night, it would be Big Buck. Always there. Always watching him. But right now, Robert needed something else.

Suddenly a high scream shattered the silence. Robert looked out. Well past the safety of the raft, the small girl's head sank beneath the water. His body froze. If he jumped in the water, his secret life would end. But if he didn't . . .

Faster than a thought, he leaped into the water. Slapping his arms flat against the surface, he swam furiously. He did not let the girl out of his sight.

Swimming beside her, he realized his mistake—too late. In panic she threw arms around him, dragging them both under the water. They struggled. He managed to unlock her arms, then spun her around by the waist. He pushed her up. Gasping, he held her chin with one hand and locked his elbow between her shoulder blades to keep her afloat.

"Calm down! I have you!" He wheezed, gulping air. He sidestroked toward shore.

Robert breathed heavier. His heart pounded inside his chest like a trapped fist trying to get out. He could not catch his breath. The girl's head slowly . . . slowly slipped from his grasp. *Not an asthma attack!*

In panic he felt her long hair slip through his fingers. His breath came back. Snapping his legs in a quick scissors kick, he righted himself in the water. Then bending in half, he dove beneath the black waters. He followed the bubbles. He held his arms in front of him in a blind search—for warmth, for hair . . . for anything.

He felt a head and quickly cupped his hand beneath her chin. He struggled upward. As they broke surface, a cheer rang out from another world. He held her head tightly against his side. He fought for air. One more stroke. He moaned. One more gulp of air, and we're home free!

A crowd of people had gathered on the beach. Robert felt fumbling hands clutch his body, dragging them both to safety. Crawling on hands and knees, he dragged himself to one side, high on the beach. He sprawled flat against the hot sand, catching his breath.

The crowd now turned their backs to him and circled

the young girl. A lifeguard gave mouth-to-mouth resuscitation. The girl choked a few times, then sat up. She was O.K. A little scared, but O.K.!

The voices sounded far away to Robert . . . so far away, as if from a closed room down the far end of a hall.

A blur broke from the crowd and headed toward him. In a daze, Robert felt two hands grab his shoulders. The blur bent closer to his face.

"Robert!" Russ Kochak prayed. "Robert, is that you?" Pulling the boy to his feet, Russ pressed him against his potbelly. "I never gave up hope, not for a minute." Russ pumped his hands until Robert thought they might fall off.

Too choked to speak, Robert nodded, beaming inside. Russ clutched his shoulders. Aimee straddled a leg. Then in the distance, as in a fog, Robert saw a familiar face shove a path through the crowd toward him. Could it be?

"Mom!" Robert screamed. His heart leaped into his throat. His mother threw both arms around him. Without speaking, they hugged each other for minutes. Robert pushed her back for a better look. Tears filled her eyes. Except for a small scar across her forehead, she looked fine. Everyone looked fine. Even the kid who had the smelly fish.

Later Russ pulled Robert to one side. Robert stood tall, nearly as tall as Russ. Russ whispered, "It won't be easy, but we'll give it another try . . . O.K.?"

Robert nodded. "We're family!"

"I mean, we're all we have."

"Don't worry, Russ. We'll make it this time." He held out a sinewy brown hand and his father grabbed it.

As the family headed for the car, Robert took a last look over his shoulder at the tangled wilderness on the other side of the lake. Through the jumble of vines and branches was Big Buck still watching him? He turned and waved as Russ put the car in gear.

ABOUT THE AUTHOR

GUS CAZZOLA is a free-lance author whose credits include books, magazines, newspaper reporting, and writing for educational services. He has served as writing judge for the New Jersey State Council of the Arts Grants Committee. Mr. Cazzola is an elementary school teacher. He and his family live in Toms River, New Jersey.